my family

my family

mahadevi varma

Introduced and translated from the Hindi by

RUTH VANITA

PENGUIN

An imprint of Penguin Random House

HAMISH HAMILTON

USA | Canada | UK | Ireland | Australia
New Zealand | India | South Africa | China

Hamish Hamilton is part of the Penguin Random House group of companies whose addresses can be found at global.penguinrandomhouse.com

Published by Penguin Random House India Pvt. Ltd
4th Floor, Capital Tower 1, MG Road,
Gurugram 122 002, Haryana, India

Penguin
Random House
India

First published in Hindi in *Mahadevi Varma Sahitya* (Collection of Mahadevi Varma's original works), Vol. No. 2, pp. 277–313 by Setu Prakashan, Jhansi, 1969
First published in English in Hamish Hamilton by Penguin Random House India 2021

Illustrations by Antra K

10 9 8 7 6 5 4 3 2 1

ISBN 9780670095902

Typeset in Adobe Caslon Pro by Manipal Technologies Limited, Manipal
Printed at Replika Press Pvt. Ltd, India

www.penguin.co.in

This translation is dedicated to Sanju Mahale,
whose home is a sanctuary for friends, dogs,
birds, and other animals

Contents

Introduction ix
Atmika (Mahadevi Varma's Preface) xxxvii

Neelkanth the Peacock 1
Gillu the Squirrel 19
Sona the Doe 29
Durmukh the Rabbit 47
Gaura the Cow 59
Neelu the Dog 71
Nikki, Rosie, and Rani 83

A Note on the Author and the Translator 105

Introduction

Mahadevi Varma is commonly acknowledged as the greatest twentieth-century woman poet in Hindi. She is often called the modern Mira, since Mirabai is Hindi's best-known woman poet across time. Mahadevi was also a prose writer of the first order and an accomplished translator, journalist, and educationist. In addition to writing, she also painted, and from 1935 to 1938, she was the unpaid volunteer editor of the famous Hindi women's magazine *Chand*.[1]

Mera Parivar (My Family) has never before been translated into English. It is the most neglected of her works, hardly mentioned by biographers and critics. As novelist Ilachandra Joshi points out, this book belongs to a new genre virtually invented by her, 'neither prose nor verse . . . nor simply a sketch'.[2] These writings are meditations in poetic prose, looking both outward at the world of all living beings, and inward at the imagination illuminated by these beings.

The genre that Mahadevi invented for autobiographical writing displaces the ego from its centre. Focusing on others, human or non-human, Mahadevi presents herself as one among many agents, the observer but also the observed. The animals whom she adopts observe and establish a relationship on their own terms with her, with each other, and with other humans. In her telling, the animals' ways of seeing are as important as human ways.

Published in 1972, this book is the last of Mahadevi's prose works. Memory runs through it and holds it together. Mahadevi ends her preface with the remarkable statement that all her prose writings stem from her writing about animals. She tells us that her first independent piece of prose was a memorandum that she, as a child, made about a chick whom she had saved from the cooking pot.

She wrote a detailed note about the chick's distinctive individual features, because she realized that if she could not remember and identify each animal, she would not be able to protect them: 'anyone could carry them away'. Thus, her body of work begins and ends with writing about animals.

Mahadevi's acclaimed portraits of humans, whether villagers, vendors, domestic workers or fellow writers, develop from her first recording of a non-human fellow being's individuality. The chicken is an individual to her, but others see it as an object that they can carry away and use or kill. Mahadevi's writings bring us face-to-face with the unforgettable individuality of animals like dogs, cats, and horses, whom we are used to thinking of as pets with personalities. However, her writings also bring us close to animals whom many people consider food products, such as chickens, or those whom humans hunt, such as deer.

When the chicken was carried away to be eaten, Mahadevi, a primary-school student, realized her own helplessness and wept inconsolably. Reporting the matter to the school matron, she referred to the chicken not as a chicken but as '*mera baccha*' (my child). The bewildered matron naturally took a while to figure out what the little girl meant. The child Mahadevi's response to the chicken as a child smaller and more helpless than herself grows into the adult Mahadevi's idea of animals as her family.

This family shapes her idea of herself, as families tend to do. *Atmika* is the lovely word Mahadevi coined as the title of her preface to this book. Twelve years later, she used the word again as the title of a book of her selected poems (1983). The word combines the idea of the spiritual (connected to the eternal self, the *atman*) with the idea of the intimate interiority of the individual self (*atmik*), both of which she feminizes.[3]

The child Mahadevi sought solitude in the orchard (where she discovered a community of living beings) because she found the bullying of older girls in her boarding school intolerable. Older girls were supposed to treat younger girls as their sisters but, in fact, ordered them around. Mahadevi's sister found ways to adapt to this, but Mahadevi rebelled.

Likewise, as an adult, Mahadevi refused to be dominated by anyone. She writes that her beloved father gave free rein to her childhood rebelliousness.

Astonishingly liberal for his time, he sent her to boarding school to get a better education, although this was unheard of in families like his. Having a supportive father is often the single most crucial factor for an Indian woman to forge ahead in any field. Being the oldest child and therefore the only child for a while also plays a role in building a girl's confidence. Mahadevi was the first girl born to her family in a couple of generations and thus was a much-desired and welcomed daughter; she was named to thank Goddess Durga.

However, her father conformed to the custom of his community by marrying her off when she was nine, mainly because he wanted to fulfil his dying father's wish to see her married.[4] As a child, Mahadevi wept continuously during the customary couple of days that she spent at her in-laws' house and had to be sent back home earlier than planned. As an adult, when the *gauna* (ceremony of departure to the husband's house) was to take place after she had graduated from college, she refused, Mirabai-like, to go and live with her husband. Her remorseful father then offered to convert along with her if she wanted to divorce her husband and remarry since

Christians and Muslims could legally divorce at the time, but Hindus could not. Mahadevi refused, saying she had no desire to remarry.

Instead, she formed her own chosen family, a large household of humans, birds, and animals. This family included those who lived in her house, from Bhaktin, the woman who turned up on her doorstep and insisted on becoming her lifelong housekeeper, to rabbits and squirrels. It also extended far beyond her home, to the great poet Nirala, whom she adopted as her brother (though he had to borrow money from her to give her as a Rakhi gift!), to her close female friends, whom she considered sisters, as well as to younger fellow writers, students in the girls' school and college that she headed, and village children, like Gheesa, whom she educated for free. All the younger people called her Guru-ji.

Mahadevi's home was a modern hermitage, where she fiercely guarded the privacy of her living quarters, although her sitting room and compound were open to all. Like the hermitages of ancient sages described in the epics, her home was a refuge for all.[5]

Mahadevi was among the most illustrious of two generations of women who, during the independence movement and the first four decades of independent India, chose to remain single and to immerse themselves in their work. These women included many educationists, teachers, and heads of girls' schools and colleges throughout the country.[6]

Immediately after earning an MA in Sanskrit, Mahadevi became the principal of Prayag Mahila Vidyapeeth, which she developed into an institution that educated girls from the primary level to the college intermediate level. Her students participated in art, music, drama, debates, and vigorous physical exercise, and, as she describes, also interacted with her animal companions.

Mahadevi soon rose to fame as one of the four pillars of the Chhayavad movement in Hindi poetry. Chhayavad (literally, shadow-ism) is an odd term used to label the movement, which dominated the two decades from the 1920s to the 1940s. The term was coined not by the poets themselves but by their critics. Mahadevi was the only woman in the group; the other three were Suryakant Tripathi 'Nirala', Sumitranandan Pant, and Jaishankar Prasad.

Although scholars have compared these poets with European Romantics and Symbolists and medieval bhakta poets, Chhayavad was a new development. The poets wrote in modern Hindi and combined an inward turn towards emotional reality with a yearning for oneness with the universe. In different ways, all four poets led difficult and unconventional lives. Pant never married and Nirala did not remarry after his wife died when he was twenty.

Until recently, single women in India were frequently portrayed in media and literature either as self-sacrificing ascetics or as unfortunate victims who face prejudices and problems. Biographies of Mahadevi often describe her as a lonely ascetic who devoted herself to the welfare of others.[7]

Mahadevi's own writings, including this book, depict the joy and freedom of being single. All those who knew her and wrote about her mention her frequent laughter and her wit. She collected art but also locally made toys, travelled and took vacations with members of her household, bought three houses, and decided her own routines. She had a faithful retinue of workers, who spared her the burden of housework, but she liked to cook and would often prepare snacks for herself and for visitors in the kitchenette adjoining the sitting room.

In this happy single life, which combined the pleasures of typical male and female existence, animals were privileged participants. Very few human friends were allowed to go beyond the sitting room into Mahadevi's study, bedroom, and other rooms. Her portraits of animals depict the varieties of intimacy that she shared with them but not with humans, facets of her life not visible to the world: her bed where Gillu the squirrel spent his last night clinging to her finger, her study, where infant peacocks were nurtured, and the dining table where she ate her meals alone except for Gillu, who ate from her plate.

'Only animals were not expelled from Paradise', remarks Milan Kundera. Mahadevi realistically depicts violence in the animal world: apart from predators, the jealous peahen and the belligerent rabbit wreak destruction. However, she does depict most of the animals' love for her as paradisal. They miss her when she travels, her dog insists on visiting her in the hospital, and all of them lavish a non-self-seeking affection on her. They form unusual friendships among themselves: a doe helps babysit puppies, a peacock rescues a baby rabbit from a snake and then warms it under his feathers until it recovers, and a dog rescues fledgelings that fall from their nests.

Kindness to Animals in Literature

Animals emerge in Mahadevi's narratives as nobler than humans. Lucy the mountain dog dies because she willingly takes risks to serve villagers, and Gaura the cow, who generously shares her milk with other animals, is murdered by a greedy milkman. Similarly, Leo Tolstoy's 'Strider: The Story of a Horse' and Mikhail Bulgakov's much later novel *Heart of a Dog* depict most humans as much more mean and vicious than animals. Mahadevi once introduced her cat as her granddaughter and her dog as her grandson, saying that humans could abandon affection and friendship born of living together, but animals could never do so.[8]

Most of Mahadevi's companion animals were rescued; their mothers were killed in the wild when they were infants.[9] The only ones she bought were caged birds, whom she set free unless their wings had been clipped, in which case she gave them shelter. Most of the animals lived both in shelters and outside them. Thus, the peacocks in the aviary were allowed out to roost on trees in her garden, the squirrel went in and out of the house at will, and the mongoose accompanied Mahadevi to school and stayed in the school garden while she was in class.

Mahadevi's concern for entrapped, hunted, and tortured animals is related to a concern for all those who are oppressed and exploited. The nineteenth century was the period that gave rise to modern movements for laws to prevent cruelty to several groups and to win rights for them. These groups include women, children, manual labourers, factory workers, prisoners, the poor, the mentally ill, and animals.

From William Blake and William Wordsworth to Thomas Hardy, many nineteenth-century European writers wrote poems lamenting such cruelties as hunting for sport, trapping for fur, encaging birds, and blinding birds because it was thought that this made them sing more sweetly. Guy de Maupassant's story 'The Donkey' is a graphic depiction of two men who torture and finally kill a donkey just for fun.

Women were at the forefront of movements against such abuse and produced much of the anti-cruelty literature that helped change laws. For example, Anna Sewell's immensely popular novel *Black Beauty* (1877), which protested against the merciless exploitation of horses, resulted in anti-cruelty legislation both in England and the US. The world's first anti-vivisection society, which worked to end cruel experiments on animals in laboratories, was founded by Francis Power Cobbe, an Irish suffragist and reformer.

Single women, in particular, wrote about their close relationships with animals. The Ladies of Llangollen, two women who lived together for fifty years in early nineteenth-century Wales and whose home became a famous centre for nature and art, wrote about their hens, dogs, and other animals as family members, giving them names, recording their lives, and burying them in marked graves.

Indian social reform movements (such as the Arya Samaj, Prarthana Samaj, and Brahmo Samaj) did not focus on animals in the same way, nor did militant, progressive, and left-wing movements, even after Independence. Mahatma Gandhi was the sole exception: his writings insisted on the rights of former untouchables (whom he termed Harijan, 'God's people', a word formerly used by bhakta poets for all devotees), women, and the poor, but also on the importance of kindness to all animals. In his ashrams, killing, even of snakes, was avoided. Gandhi's thinking about animals was shaped by Hindu and Jain philosophy but also by his association with vegetarian and anti-vivisection movements when he was a student in London.

Mahadevi was a devoted follower of Gandhi. As a student, she took significant risks to carry secret letters and papers between militant revolutionaries, but later, after travelling to various pilgrimage places, such as Badrinath, Rameshwar, Puri, visiting the ashrams of Ramana Maharishi and Gandhi, and considering and rejecting the option of becoming a Buddhist nun, she joined the Gandhi-led independence movement. She removed her gold and silver jewellery and burnt the expensive, spangled clothes inherited from her mother and grandmothers. She took and kept the pledge to wear khadi all her life and followed the advice Gandhi gave her, to teach poor women to read and write in their mother tongue. She also helped freedom fighters in every way she could, selling her dressing table to donate money, hiding paperwork and lithograph machines from the police, carrying messages and food for rebels. When Ilachandra Joshi warned her that getting arrested was especially risky for women, she answered that she was a true inheritor of the tradition of *jauhar* and would not be taken alive.[10]

Like Gandhi, she inherited her vegetarianism from her mother, even though her father, a typical Kayastha man, ate flesh and enjoyed hunting. It was, and still is, a pattern in many households for men to eat non-vegetarian food outside the house while women prefer to remain vegetarian. Mahadevi's vegetarianism was based on her experience as well as her philosophy.

Her thinking with regard to animals draws on both Indian and Western literature. Chhayavad was strongly influenced both by Upanishadic thought and by English Romanticism. Romantic and Transcendental writers had drawn on the

Upanishads, the Bhagavad Gita, and other Sanskrit works, which were first translated into English in the eighteenth century. Henry David Thoreau directly cites Indian literature in his musings about animals and rebirth.[11] It was, therefore, natural for Indian readers to be strongly drawn to English Romantic poetry.

Romantic and Victorian writers often celebrate the oneness of all living beings and the divine spirit that animates them: 'a motion and a spirit that impels/ All thinking things, all objects of all thought/ And rolls through all things'.[12] Both Goethe and Percy Shelley greatly admired Kalidasa's depiction of Shakuntala's closeness to deer and to plants, a scene that Mahadevi too quotes when describing her doe.

Indian literature has a long tradition, dating back to the Panchatantra and the Ramayana, of depicting animal characters as moral agents with innate value, dignity, and agency. This tradition continues in medieval literature, for example, in Marathi devotional poet Bahinabai's moving account of her attachment to her cow and calf. Although less common in modern Indian literature, it does appear, for example, in Tagore's *Streer Patra*, where the abused wife, like Bahinabai, finds sympathetic friends only in the cows and calves.[13] Western literature, especially in the modern period, relegates speaking animal characters largely to children's literature. For example, *Black Beauty* was written for and read by adults but is now treated as children's literature.

Twentieth-century Indian writers, eager to prove their modern humanist credentials, tend to adopt dominant colonial views and therefore do not depict animals as having agency. There are several outstanding exceptions, such as Premchand's story 'Two Bullocks' and, much later, in a different vein, Suniti Namjoshi's *Conversations of Cow*. Awareness of animal consciousness and suffering increased steadily in literature throughout the twentieth century, from the writings of Nobel Prize winners Isaac Bashevis Singer and J.M. Coetzee to those of Virginia Woolf and Milan Kundera.

Mahadevi calls her animals *sangi* and *saathi*, companions rather than pets. She notices differences between species—deer are not servile or submissive as many dogs are; cows, even though humans mistreat them, retain their calm confidence. Like humans, animals are shaped not just by innate traits but by individual experience. She notes that the mountain dog Neelu, whose mother was not owned by anyone, is loyal like all dogs but has a unique dignity, taking offence if he is scolded and refusing food that is thrown to him. She wonders whether Durmukh, the ill-tempered rabbit, would have been less aggressive had he not suffered the trauma in infancy of his entire family being killed by a cat.

Dhwani, Memory, and Modernity

Mahadevi wrote three other books of pen portraits. Two are of ordinary people she encountered, mostly poor people, including domestic workers, vendors, and rural women, men, and children. The third portrays contemporary writers, whom she terms companions on the road (*path ke saathi*).

The remarkable mix of playfulness and profundity in Mahadevi's prose was hard for me to reproduce in English, partly because she employs philosophical concepts, such as *samskara*,[14] in unexpected, often semi-humorous contexts, and partly because of the way she combines Sanskrit words with local words and seemingly strange but oddly imaginative adjectives with everyday nouns, for example, *'udasin-sa nilkantha'* and *'chakit-sa kauva'*. Her flexible style ranges from the humorous, as when the children think that white ponies are donkeys, based on the stories they have heard, to a kind of lyrical beauty based on intensely noticed detail, as when she describes the white cow and her red calf: *'mata-putra donon nikat rahne par himrashi aur jalte angaare ka smaran karate the'* (When mother and son were together, they reminded one of snow and fire) or the peacock dancing: *'Aage-peechhe daahine-baa'en kram se ghoomkar voh kisi alakshya sam par thahar-thahar jata tha'* (As he stepped forward and backward, left and right, he would pause at some invisible point where rhythms meet). Although she remarks that words and pictures cannot convey movement, her words bring before one's eyes the distinctly different way in which each animal moves, looks, acts, and reacts. The inherently magical, mysterious nature of the world animates her prose.

'Gillu' has sometimes been simplified and turned into a children's story, but the plangent style of these sketches, contemplative, witty, and satirical, is not geared towards children. Mahadevi has a penchant for understated but biting satire; for example, the caged birds and rabbits suffer outside an overcrowded government hospital, and inside, the poor often die while they wait to see a doctor. The author does not compare the two; she simply juxtaposes them and remarks on the satisfaction the poor derive merely from dying within the hospital precincts.

Mahadevi's language is replete with what is known in Indian poetics as *dhwani* or resonance, suggestiveness. The reader must be *sahridaya* (literally, of one heart), sharing the emotions and sensitivities of the writer, to catch some less obvious resonances. Take the sentence describing a peahen waiting for her dead mate: *'Radha ab pratiksha mein hi dukeli hai'*. The Sanskrit word *pratiksha* (waiting) combines with the untranslatable Hindi word *dukela* (alone together), feminized as *dukeli*. It is obvious that the peahen Radha's grief recalls Krishna's beloved, Radha, left pining in the village after he went to the city, never to return. A less obvious suggestion in the word *dukeli* is that like Radha, a goddess who is ever one with Krishna, the peahen Radha is both alone and not alone because she is united with her beloved in her heart.

Most mystic poets, such as Mirabai, dwell on this simultaneous separation from and union with the divine. In Mahadevi's poetry, too, the female speaker constantly expresses her paradoxical distance from and oneness with an unspecified and unnamed beloved:

ek karun abhaav mein chir-
tripti ka sanchaar sanchit
ek laghu kshan de raha
nirvaan ke vardaan shat shat

paa liya maine kise iss
vedna ke madhur kray mein?
kaun tum mere hriday mein?[15]

Holding eternal satisfaction
in the flow of this one sad absence,
Giving the blessing of liberation
Hundreds of times in each short moment,

Whom have I obtained
In the sweet laments of sorrow?
Who are you in my heart?

The peacock waiting for the rain clouds is a favourite Indian mystical image for the devotee-lover awaiting union with the divine beloved. Mahadevi gives this image a twist when she identifies the peahen as the lover. The peacock also recalls Radha's beloved, Krishna, crowned with a peacock feather.

Mahadevi's deep immersion in classical Indian literature goes hand in hand with local belief and feeling. Thus, along with her analysis of Durmukh the rabbit's trauma in infancy as the cause of his aggressiveness, she also records her gardener's decided opinion that Durmukh's valour was due to the influence or spirit (*chhaya*) of a local wrestler (*pahalwan-ji*), to whose tomb (*samadhi*) villagers from near and far came to make wishes. Both these views suggest that humans and other animals are more similar than different.

This book is based in individual memory but also in collective memory. Mahadevi records a kind of Indian urban modernity that encompasses ways of interacting with nature that are now gradually disappearing. Her writing brings to life a world where boundaries between human and non-human life, urban and rural, are permeable. This world survives today in smaller towns and even in many outlying areas of big cities. Before milk was sold in plastic or cardboard containers or even in bottles, a milkman would bring it in cans to the door and measure it out into household pitchers or even milk a buffalo at the door. When air-conditioning is not ubiquitous, doors and windows are often left open. This allows birds to build nests on ceiling fans, inside air coolers, in skylights and other niches, and in bathroom flush tanks of the old kind. Mongooses and snakes make their way into the house and slumber in dark corners, while monkeys enter homes through open windows and go to bathrooms to cool down with water or to kitchens to help themselves to food.

Mahadevi concludes her book by recalling how boarding school exiled her into the land of adult common sense. Perhaps it is because her exiled self never lost touch with the uncommon sense of a child that she wrote about animals in an unmatched way. Like many poets, she retains something of the child's vision that does not discriminate among living beings: 'Children do not perceive different levels of consciousness; they perceive just one consciousness. For them, animals, birds, and plants all belong to one family' ('Nikki, Rosie, and Rani'). This view of all beings as manifestations of one consciousness is an Upanishadic view.

Ruth Vanita

Notes

1. While it is customary in English to refer to writers by their second names, I here refer to her by her first name, the way she is usually referred to in Hindi. Her name means 'great Goddess' and has a more powerful resonance than her father's name, Varma. A good biography is *Mahiyasi Mahadevi* (Allahabad: Lokbharti Prakashan, 1969) by Mahadevi's close associate Ganga Prasad Pande.
2. Joshi, Foreword to *Mera Parivar* (Allahabad: Lokbharti Prakashan, 1972; 2019), pp. 5–10; 10. All translations in this introduction are by me.
3. 'Atmika', I notice, has come into fashion lately as a name for girls, and is the title of a 2010 short film.

4. Marxist critic Doodhnath Singh speculates wildly that Mahadevi's father married her off when he was working in the Narsinghgarh princely state because Mahadevi may have started a romance with a Muslim officer at the palace. The evidence he offers for this is that Mahadevi frequently visited her close friend, Queen Shivrani Devi, at the palace, that Mahadevi had the reputation of being obstinate, that Mahadevi was a very private person and never wrote about her experiences in Narsinghgarh, and that the one person Singh spoke to suggested the idea of this romance to him. Singh, *Mahadevi* (New Delhi: Rajkamal Prakashan, 2009), pp. 256–61.
5. This comparison occurred to Ganga Prasad Pande when he first met her and saw her cat and dog playing together. Pande, *Mahiyasi Mahadevi*, p. 49.
6. I interviewed some of these remarkable women in the 1980s for *Manushi*, India's first nationwide feminist magazine of which I was founding co-editor. One was Kanti Shastri, lecturer at Miranda House, who was active in the freedom movement and later with Ram Manohar Lohia and in the Sarvodaya movement in the 1950s–'60s. See 'Education and Independence: An interview with Kanti Shastri', *Manushi* No. 44 (1988), pp. 11–20.
7. According to Doodhnath Singh, all Mahadevi's actions, from her writings to her Vedantic pilgrimages to her Gandhian social welfare activities to her habit of breaking into laughter, were attempts to escape her depression (p. 269). He considers the residents of Indian princely

states as more 'uneducated, backward-looking and subjugated' than the residents of 'the new world', that is, the territories colonized by the British (p. 262), and claims that Mahadevi never managed to get liberated from the familial influence of the Arya Samaj and Vedic knowledge (p. 264). He repeatedly states that all Mahadevi's writings, especially her poems, are a 'scream' (*cheetkaar*, pp. 57, 257, 258) expressing the 'repressed longing for love' (p. 63) and the grief, fear and bondage of all twentieth-century Indian women (p. 57). This is a prime though later example of what Pande terms 'the laughable attempts of male and female devotees of Freud' to explain Mahadevi's personality and writings on the basis of their invented allegations' (Pande, pp. 31–32), even though Mahadevi defined poetry as 'the acceptance of affection for the universe' (p. 32). Similarly, Anita Anantharam assumes that unsatisfied heterosexual eroticism, which she politely terms Mahadevi's 'personal longing for fulfilment as a woman' (p. 14) and 'longing for companionship' (p. 13), fuel Mahadevi's poetry. Anantharam, ed., *Mahadevi Varma: Political Essays on Women, Culture and Nation* (Amherst, NY: Cambria Press, 2010). Anantharam does not mention *Mera Parivar*, and neither she nor Singh takes seriously Mahadevi's own accounts of her companionship with animals.

8. Pande, p. 50.
9. Pande recounts how as a child, Mahadevi wept aloud until she was allowed to bring some stray puppies

into the house one winter night. He writes that all her life, she continued to host such animal guests (Pande, p. 26).

10. Pande, p. 57. When defeat at the hands of Muslim rulers became inevitable, north Indian Hindu men in the medieval period, both Rajputs and others, would rush to certain death in battle; this was known as *shaka*. Women would collectively enter the fire to avoid enslavement and rape; this was known as jauhar.
11. See Vanita, 'Birds, Cows and Rebirth in Thoreau and Tagore', forthcoming in the journal *Sophia*.
12. William Wordsworth, 'Lines Written a few Miles above Tintern Abbey', 1798.
13. See Vanita, '"I'm an Excellent Animal": Cows at Play in the Writings of Bahinabai, Suniti Namjoshi, and Others', in Vanita, *Gandhi's Tiger and Sita's Smile: Essays on Gender, Sexuality and Culture* (New Delhi: Yoda Press, 2005), and '"The Comprehensiveness of Sympathy": Gender and Species in Tagore', forthcoming in *Essays on English and Indian Literature: A Festschrift for G.K. Das*, edited by R.W. Desai et al. (New Delhi: Aakar Books).
14. The word 'samskara' has more than one meaning. It refers to the impressions or memory-traces carried by each self from former births, which become personal predilections. It also refers to impressions received in childhood, which affect one's personality (similar to English 'social conditioning'). Life-cycle rituals, such as

naming, initiation, wedding and death ceremonies are also called samskara.

15. From Mahadevi's poem '*Kaun tum mere hriday mein?*' Translation mine.

Atmika[1]

Animals and birds have been my primary companions on memory's journey, but, unfortunately, humans have easily seized this primacy from them.

In 1918, when I entered Crossthwaite Girls' College as a class five student, my enthusiasm for education was greater than my distress at being far from home. Yet, as my heart's dissonance with that atmosphere kept increasing, my distress too continued to escalate.

At that time, two big and two small girl students shared each room in the student residence. This arrangement was probably inspired by the kindly desire for older students to look after their younger sisters and for the younger girls to remain within the disciplinary boundaries set by their older sisters. However, the results of this imbalanced arrangement could not be pleasant for the little girls. The unfamiliarity of newness heightened the natural shyness induced by being the youngest. The weight of this doubled novelty made some of the little girls rebellious and frustrated others. Sometimes willingly and sometimes unwillingly, they had to clean the desks, chairs, and cupboards in the room and perform tasks, such as bringing in the older students' clothes that were dried on the line outside and fetching tea and snacks for them. Entertaining the older girls by singing and dancing when commanded to do so, and even by posturing as cocks, was their duty.[2] Clearly, this situation was hard for me to tolerate.

Work came within the definition of *seva* (service), so an innate, inherited satisfaction accompanied it. But to undertake a variety of efforts simply to amuse someone gave rise to wordless anger.

My sister, Shyama, was different from me in this regard. She thought that though it was impossible to cry or lament when ordered, singing could be considered as natural as to look or to hear. Do our eyes and ears wait for anyone's orders to see or to hear? Also, dancing and singing could work as weapons. Someone can tell you to sing, but no one can tell you to make your voice more melodious. One can sing in an untuneful manner like a donkey, which will make listeners cover their ears and run away, and as for dance, one can spin in a way that will make the spectators' heads spin. I had no answer to this logic or illogic, but I have never been able to use the weapons of others. Incompatibility with the environment made my heart, like the pendulum of a clock, move at full speed to the rhythm of home, father, mother, younger brothers, and Rama.[3] This rotation of memories began to disturb my mind with worries about the animals and birds that I had reared.

Intensity of experience leaves an imprint on the world of our hearts, and this intensity does not depend on the importance or triviality of our experiences. A child's experience of sorrow when a toy breaks can be more intense and real than an adult's grief at parting from a dear one. That is why the joys and sorrows of childhood are especially important to psychologists.

On the western boundary of the college was an orchard of mango, guava, lime, and jackfruit trees, which a market-gardener woman had taken on contract. It was only when the absence of that orchard made everything seem empty and bleak to me that I realized how my heart, wandering in search of a congenial environment, had found in it a resting place.

A few boughs of a mango tree were so low that it was easy to sit on them. As soon as classes were over, I would collect paper, pens, and books and go to sit on the mango boughs, sometimes swinging my legs and sometimes cross-legged in a *padmasana* posture. It was necessary to keep a book open in front of me to reassure myself, but what I most enjoyed reading moved about around me, freed from the book's imprisonment. When we see a person in front of us, do we open a book to get information about the person's nose, ears, and eyes?

The woman gardener's three black, naked children hid behind the tree for a couple of days, watching me with curiosity. Then, as if recognizing me by human odour as belonging to the same tribe as themselves, they gradually began to come closer. They would shyly touch my clothes or else hang from the boughs in a manner that afforded me the pleasure of being on a swing. The woman gardener had reared a speckled goat and a yellow-beaked white hen. After some days of suspiciously keeping her distance, the goat began to sit beneath the boughs while the hen hopped about, making the ground and the lower branches one. It now became necessary to bring some bread from the hostel or buy some sweets from the sweet-vending woman for all these companions. The woman gardener, too, would contribute a guava or lime now and then, and sometimes a handful of roasted chickpeas or a lump of raw sugar.

The teachers and boarders were highly impressed by my studious habits. Such a young student in a primary class, so dedicated to reading and writing! She had no time to play and no eagerness to eat. She even considered talking a waste of time. They thought my studies were no less than austerities because in their view, the garden breezes spread the stink of the goat and hen, the gardener's dirty, naked children were a noisy crew, and the dried yellow leaves that fell were a nuisance.

No one perceived the beauty with which my heart had become acquainted. In spring, when the mango tree was laden with golden blossoms, the cuckoo called, hidden among the leaves on a higher branch. Swinging on a lower branch, I would imitate that cry and she would reply,[4] while the gardener's three children would clap, assuming the role of curious spectators.

When fruit appeared on the mango and guava trees, flocks of parrots would sit in rows on the branches, creating the illusion of a festoon of fruits suspended over a doorway. As each gust blew, it showered down the mingled, bittersweet perfumes of mango and lime flowers. Now and then, a detached-seeming peacock or an apparently surprised crow would alight on a mango sprout. Flocks of sparrows and other tiny birds kept up a non-stop chirruping.

Rays of sunlight filtered through the dense, playful mango leaves and quivered as they fell. Looking at them felt as if some unseen gardener were watering the mango branches from above with golden water in a sapphire watering can, and those sparkling drops were flowing down, forming golden streaks.

That was the spring I saw the white hen, with puffed-out wings, accompanying her five children who looked like balls of silk-cotton. Like most Hindu homes, ours had never reared hens, so those chicks were such a novelty to me that I forgot my other companions and centred my attention on them.[5]

As soon as I reached the orchard, I would first count the hen's children. Then I would pick up each one, wipe it with my handkerchief from beak to claws, and enthrone myself on the mango branches only after scattering millet or some other grain for them.

One day, the fifth chicken was not to be seen. When I inquired, the woman gardener told me that the new Miss Saheb who had come to live in the student hostel had taken it away. I wondered how she would manage to look after such a small creature. The gardener naturally laughed at my ignorance, but I wouldn't be surprised if the anguish I experienced when she expanded my knowledge left a mark on me that I feel even today.

When the gardener told me that the small, tender-bodied chicken would give its life to increase the number of Miss Saheb's delicacies, I, for the first time, wept from sheer helplessness. The matron was especially fond of me, so she grew worried when I refused to eat and kept crying. It took her a while to understand what I meant when I said, 'The new Miss Saheb has killed and eaten my child.' As it happened, the baby chicken was to be converted into a delicacy at dinner time so the cook had kept it in a small, closed basket.

That day, I got the baby chicken back and returned him to his mother. But after that, a nameless fear took hold of me. If I could not keep track of the numbers and identifying marks of my non-human friends, anyone could take them away. I had no other way to prove that I was their protector.

First of all, I wrote down the identifying marks of the chick who had returned from death's door.

Number Five: colour, a yellowish-white, eyes round and red like a ruby, beak pink-edged with yellow streaks, dark red claws with white nails, walks with a staggering gait. His feathers are somewhat sprouted, edged with dark red dots. He can eat millet or broken rice.

He was named Munga (Coral).

In this manner, I wrote down the number, colours, special marks, and names of all the animals and birds. At that time, I did not know that in the future, the practice of this kind of memorandum-keeping would become habitual to me. But all my memoirs have sprouted, budded, and bloomed from this childhood prose expression of mine.

Mahadevi
15 May 1972

Notes

1. The author's preface in the original Hindi book.
2. Posturing as a cock refers to squatting down, placing one's head between one's knees, and looping the arms behind the knees to hold the ears. Teachers in north India used to punish offending children by making them assume this position.
3. Rama looked after Mahadevi and her siblings in their early childhood. A pen portrait of him appears in Mahadevi's book *Ateet ke Chalchitra* (Moving Pictures of the Past).
4. It is the male cuckoo who calls, but Mahadevi genders the bird feminine here.

5. Until the mid-twentieth century, many Hindus did not eat chickens, considering them omnivorous scavengers like pigs, and therefore dirty.

Neelkanth the Peacock

Nakkhas Kona has a strange position in the peaceful and cultural hermitage city of Prayag. Most riots and knife fights have their inauspicious beginnings in Nakkhas Kona.

It has some other special features too. Shops that sharpen everything from the large and wide blades of grass-cutting machines to hatchets, axes, saws, and knives are found here, so one need not travel far to get serrated knives and pocket knives sharpened. The government eye hospital is also in this neighbourhood. If one's ability to distinguish friends from foes is weak, one can get one's vision repaired here to avoid making mistakes. Another hospital, too, holds a proud historical place here.

It has special provisions for injured and dying people. If they do not find a place in the hospital's interior and cannot meet a doctor or nurse, they can rest in the verandas and porticoes, and if even those are too crowded, they can at least have the satisfaction of dying in the hospital's compound.

In our country, hospitals exist to provide satisfaction to ordinary people on their last journey. After being dragged to a hospital and made to hang around, when they are somehow brought within its boundary walls, invalids obtain an indescribable inner contentment, as do their caretakers. They neither imagine nor demand anything more than this. At least this system resolves the problem of having to put Ganga water, tulsi or gold in the dying person's mouth.

There are fish shops in this area and shops selling oils and perfumes, too, to maintain a balance between stench and scent.

But these are not the features that attract me to Nakkhas Kona. This place is also a prison for my rabbits, pigeons, peacocks, partridges and other living beings. On the pavement in front of the hospital are many small houses and verandas, where these beings and their hard-hearted jailors live.

In the verandas and outside them are kept many small and big cages, in which twenty-five rabbits occupy a space meant for two, and fifty birds a space meant for four. These little beings are not able to make different sounds to laugh and to cry. Their loud and sweet twittering may well be a loud lamentation. Even though I cannot think of any way to lessen the pain of these living beings, I can't stop myself from approaching them. If I see a cage without water, I make arrangements to have water put into it. If there is not enough grain, I see that more grain is provided. I buy some birds and set them free. I bring home those whose wings have been clipped. But the next time I go there, I find everything just as agonizing as it was before.

That day, I had dropped off a guest at the railway station and was returning home when I thought of the shops selling birds and rabbits and instructed the driver to take that route.

As soon as we approached Bade Miyan's shop, he came on to the road and beckoned the driver to stop. Before I could ask a question, he started off,

'Salaam Guru-ji! The last time you came, you asked about peachicks. A fowler has brought two peachicks from Shankar Garh—one is a peacock and the other a peahen. Please rear them. People make medicines from peacock claws, so those are the only buyers I have had. But I have a human heart in my breast. How can I give away such innocent chicks to be killed? To get rid of the buyers, I said, "Guru-ji has asked for them." This is a wretched profession. Nothing but catch and catch, kill and kill.'

The express train of Bade Miyan's speech has no appointed stations. Wherever the listener gets tired and stops him is a station. Since I knew this, I interrupted and asked, 'Where are the peachicks?' Following the wave of his hand, my eyes fell on a small wire cage in which two partridge-like chicks were sitting. It was hard to believe they were peacocks. The cage was so small that those chicks looked like a picture in a round netted frame.

The train of Bade Miyan's speech accompanied my inspection. 'On my honour, Guru-ji, the fowler took thirty rupees in cash from me for this pair of peacocks. I kept saying to him, "Brother, just think about it—these two show no sign of being peacocks, and you're demanding such a high price!" But why would he listen? Thinking of you, I had to force myself to pay his price. Now it's up to you.' After paying thirty in the name of the fowler and five towards Bade Miyan's honour, when I put that small cage in the car, the picture in the netting frame came alive. The two chicks fluttered so much that it seemed as if the cage had become animate and able to fly.

When we reached home, everyone said, 'They are partridges; you've been cheated into buying them as peacocks.'

Having been cheated many times, getting annoyed at the idea of being cheated has become my weakness. Displeased, I said, 'Are peacocks dipped in gold or what? Are partridges and quails worth nothing just because they don't have long tails?' Perhaps because I was irritated on their account, I made special efforts on behalf of the two birds.

First, I brought their cage into my study and opened the cage door. Then I put out two small bowls, one with small balls of coarse flour, the other with water. The chicks stepped out of the mousetrap-like cage and seemed to get lost in the room, sometimes under the desk, sometimes behind the cupboard. Finally, tiring of this hide-and-seek, they paid my wastepaper basket the honour of making it their new home. For a few days, they continued in this way, hiding during the daytime and appearing in the wastepaper basket at night. Once they grew comfortable, they began to manifest themselves, sometimes on my desk, sometimes on the chair and sometimes on my head. Were they to roam freely, my cat Chitra would get to know about these newcomers, and it was not hard to guess what the result of her investigations would be. Normally, she doesn't even attack mice, but here two absolutely unknown birds were in question. For the door to be closed to her while two vagabonds (as they would seem to her) made my desk their throne would be intolerable to a feline as conscious of her dignity as Chitra was.

When my room showed signs of being transformed into an aviary, I caught the two birds with great difficulty and took them to the big wire house where most of my creatures lived.

The two newcomers aroused great curiosity among the earlier residents, as is natural in a family when a new bride arrives. The fantail pigeons gave up dancing and began to run in circles, cooing loudly. The big rabbits sat in a row like civilized council members and gravely inspected them. The small rabbits bounced around them like woolly balls. The parrots, as if to improve their scrutiny, gazed at them with one eye closed. The rooster descended from his perch, spread out his wings and created a racket. That day an earthquake seemed to shake my aviary.

The two peachicks began to grow. Their metamorphosis proceeded as colourfully as that of a caterpillar into a butterfly.

The peacock's crest became thicker, taller and shinier. His beak grew curved and sharp, and the azure radiance of sapphires glowed in his round eyes. Waves like shot-silk, or like sunshine and shadow, rose and fell with every movement of his long blue-green throat. Grey and white patterns appeared on his wings. His tail grew longer, and rainbow-hued eyes gleamed on its feathers. His proud gait invested his colourless feet with a new majesty. The grace and beauty in his various movements when he lifted his neck to look about, bent it at an angle to pick up grain or drink water or crooked it to listen to sounds could only be experienced by watching him. Movement cannot be sketched in a picture.

The peahen's development was not miraculous like the peacock's. Still, her long, variegated neck, her crest playing in the breeze, her feathers etched with black and white, and her slow movements declared her a fit companion for him.

Because of his blue throat, the peacock was named Neelkanth, and the peahen who behaved like his shadow was named Radha.[1]

I don't quite know when Neelkanth appointed himself the commander and protector of all those living in the aviary. In the morning, he would collect his army of rabbits, pigeons and others and lead them to the place where grain was provided, and then walk around them as if protecting them. If anyone created a problem, he would rush to punish the troublemaker with an attack of his sharp beak.

He would pick up the mischievous baby rabbits by one ear with his beak and carry them around until they cried aloud. Sometimes, his sharp beak would complete the ritual of piercing the baby rabbits' ears, after which they would never again give him cause for complaint. His love for these creatures was just as extraordinary as his punitive measures. He would often sit down in the dust with his wings spread out, and they all would play catch-as-catch-can in his long tail and thick wings.

One day we received surprising evidence of his parental affection. Sometimes the rabbits and pigeons would attract snakes, and if any of the drainage pipes in the aviary remained open it would be easy for snakes to gain entrance. By some such mischance, a snake got into the aviary.

All the creatures ran and took shelter, but the snake caught one small rabbit. In trying to swallow it, the snake compressed the rabbit's hindquarters in its mouth. The squeals issuing from the half of the rabbit that was still outside were not strong enough to be heard clearly. Neelkanth was asleep on the swing high above. From there, his alert ears picked up the distress in that soft sound and, gathering up his tail and wings, he descended in one swoop.

Probably he intuitively understood that if he attacked the snake's hood directly, the rabbit could get injured. He pressed the snake down, with his claws near its hood, and attacked it with his beak until it was half-dead. As soon as its grip relaxed, the rabbit came out of its mouth but lay still as if unconscious.

Radha did not think it necessary to help, but with deep cries she announced the news of some unusual event to all and sundry. The gardener reached there first and then the rest of us. After cutting the snake in half, Neelkanth went to the baby rabbit and warmed it under his wings all night long.

Observing that bird's form and nature, one could understand why Kartikeya chose the peacock as his martial vehicle.[2]

The peacock is an art-loving, heroic bird, not simply a violent one. That is why he cannot be placed in the same category with kites, hawks, and falcons whose life consists of cruel actions. Neelkanth had the characteristics of his tribe but had also acquired some human ones. When he spread out his rainbow-like feathers into a circle and danced beneath the dusky shadow of the clouds, there was a natural rhythm and harmony to his dance. As he stepped forward and backward, left and right, he would pause at some invisible point where rhythms meet.

Radha could not dance as Neelkanth did, but there was a measure in her gait too. When Neelkanth was absorbed in his dance, she would touch his right wing and come around to his left side, then touch his left wing and come around to his right. In this way, her circumambulations had a complementary rhythm to his. I cannot say how Neelkanth came to know that I liked his dancing very much, but one day, as soon as I approached the aviary, he suddenly descended from his swing and, spreading out the circular rainbow umbrella of his feathers, he stood in a dance pose. After that, this dance pose became his everyday routine. Often there would be an Indian or foreign guest with me, and they would be amazed by Neelkanth's pose, thinking it a compliment paid to them. Several foreign ladies gave him the title of 'perfect gentleman'.[3]

With the same sharp, pointed beak that could cut a terrifying, poisonous snake to pieces, he would pick roasted chickpeas from my palm and eat them so delicately that I felt both amused and astonished.

He preferred flowering, blooming trees to fruit-laden ones. In spring, when mango trees were heavy

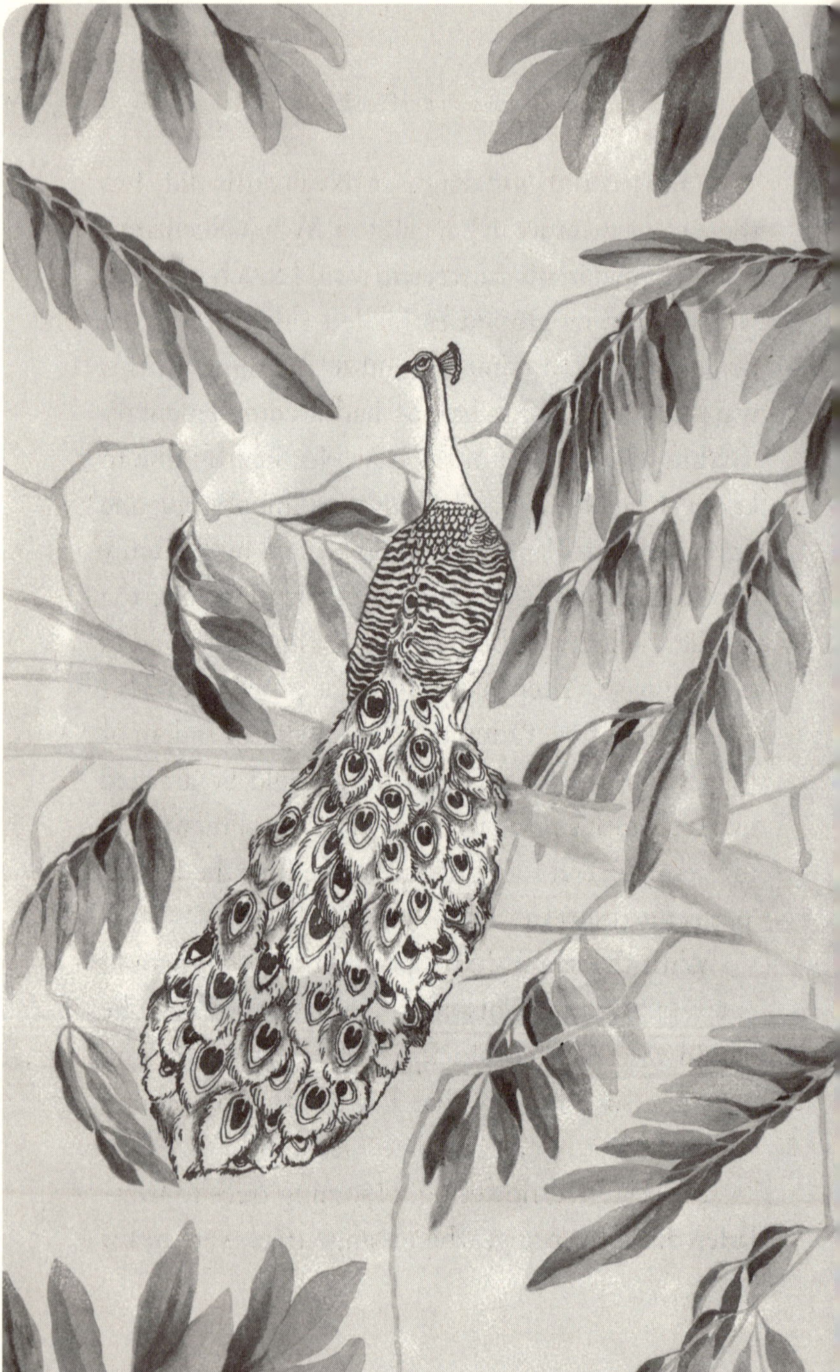

with golden blossom and the Ashoka with fresh, red flowers, he would become so agitated in the aviary that he had to be let out. But until Radha was released as well, he would stand near the door in a reproachful manner. In the twilight shadows, his sapphire glow among the flowers created an illusion, as it were, of blue lotuses in a golden pond. In the waving fronds of the Ashoka's ruddy leaves, he looked like a picture made of emeralds on a coral medallion.

The rainy season was Neelkanth and Radha's favourite time of year. Even before a cloud billowed up, they felt its moist steps in the breeze, and their resonant, deep cries would grow ever more impetuous as if building a flight of stairs for the drops to descend. His absorbed dance would keep pace with the clouds' growling. Then, as the clouds thundered more loudly, the lightning flashed more brightly, and the drops fell faster, Neelkanth's dance would pick up speed and his cry would grow increasingly insistent. When the rain stopped, he would spread out his right wing on his right foot and his left wing on his left foot, in order to dry them. Sometimes the two would dry one another's wings by drinking the drops that dripped from the other's feathers.

And now for the sad story of how a discordant note disturbed this festive melody.

One day I had to pass through Nakkhas Kona on some errand, and Bade Miyan once again stopped my car. Determined not to look at any cage today, I kept my eyes fixed on Bade Miyan's sparse beard and the spectacles secured to his ears with white cords. But it was hard to avoid seeing the peahen lying near Bade Miyan's feet. She was a lot like Radha. Her feet were tied with grass cords, and her toes were so broken and bunched up that she was not able to stand.

Bade Miyan's speech train was running once more. 'Look, Guru-ji, what that wretched fowler has done to the poor thing. Is this any way to catch a bird? Had you not come, I'd have thrown her back in his face. But how can I ask even you to take this half-dead peahen?'

To make a long story short, I paid seven rupees, had her put on the front seat, brought her home and once more turned my study into a hospital. Her feet were treated, she was taken care of, and she recovered within a month. Her toes remained crooked, but she began to hobble along on her stump-like feet. Then she was taken to the aviary and named Kubja.[4] In accordance with her name, her temperament turned out to be crooked too.

Until then, Neelkanth and Radha were always together. Now, whenever she saw them together, Kubja would run to attack Radha. Repeatedly striking her with her beak, she would tear at Radha's crest and feathers. The problem was that Neelkanth avoided Kubja, and she wanted to be with him. She had no friends among the other animals, and she did not want any of them to come near Neelkanth. Meanwhile, Radha laid two eggs and sat on them, covering them with her wings. As soon as she found out about this, Kubja pecked and pecked at Radha, pushed her away, broke the eggs and scattered the pieces all around with her stump-like feet.

When we shut her up separately, she stopped eating and drinking and kept hitting her head on the wire netting until she injured herself.

All this conflict and, what was worse, being separated from Radha put paid to poor Neelkanth's happiness. He ran away from the aviary on several occasions. Once he hid for days among the branches of the mango tree, without food or drink. With great difficulty, I coaxed him into descending. Another time, he hid on the shade that overhung my window.

When I went to feed them grain, he would stand as usual, spreading out his feathers, but his eyes seemed empty, and his gait had slowed down. Due to my inexperience, I kept hoping that as time passed, they would all begin to get along with each other. Finally, after three or four months, I found Neelkanth sitting on the ground one morning, with his tail and wings spread out as he used to do when hiding baby rabbits under his wings. But I grew anxious when he did not respond to my call.

Neelkanth was dead. I have never found out why. He was not ill, nor did we find any sign of injury on his body that was like a bunch of multicoloured flowers. I wrapped him in my shawl and carried him to the *sangam*, where the rivers meet. When he was set afloat in the middle of the Ganga, his moon-shaped feathers, reflected in a wide swathe of the Ganga, shimmered like a vast peacock.

After Neelkanth's passing, Radha sat inactive in a corner for several days. He had often run away and come back, so she seemed to be waiting, her eyes fixed on the doorway. But Kubja was loud and clamorous in her searching. As soon as the wire door was opened in the morning, she would set out to search for Neelkanth in the branches of the mango, Ashoka, *kachnar*, and other trees. One day, when she descended from the mango tree, Kajli, the Alsatian bitch, was standing below it. As was her habit, she attacked Kajli with her beak. Kajli's two teeth met in her neck. This time, her life, filled with hate, love and conflict, could not be saved. But what these three birds taught me about the diversity of birds' natures holds a special significance for me.

Now Radha is alone yet coupled in her waiting. In the month of Ashadha, when the sky is overshadowed with clouds, she sometimes sits on the high swing and sometimes on the Ashoka's branches, crying out with increasing intensity, calling Neelkanth.[5]

Notes

1. Neelkanth (Blue-Throated) is one of Shiva's names, because his throat turned blue when he held in it a deadly

poison meant to destroy all mortals. The word 'neelkanth' is also one of the words for 'peacock'.

2. Shiva's son Kartikeya (also known as Murugan) is a commander of armies.
3. These words are in English in the original.
4. Meaning, crooked. There are several stories about crooked or hunchbacked women in Sanskrit texts, most famously the woman in the Ramayana who incites her mistress to exile Rama, thus setting the plot in motion.
5. There are a couple of suggestive resonances here. Weddings are not supposed to be performed during the month of Ashadha (22 June to 22 July) in the Hindu calendar. The name of the tree, Ashoka, means 'without sorrow'.

Gillu the Squirrel

A yellow bud has appeared today on the golden jasmine creeper. This sight spontaneously calls to mind that little being who used to sit hidden in the thick greenery of this creeper and startle me by jumping on to my shoulder as soon as I drew near. In those days, I sought buds, but today, I seek that little life.

He must now be one with the earth in which this creeper is rooted. Perhaps he has risen up in the form of this golden bud in order to startle me.

One day, I stepped out from the room on to the veranda and suddenly saw two crows hopping around a flowerpot as if playing tag with their beaks. It's a strange bird, the crow—both respected and disrespected, highly honoured and highly dishonoured.

Our poor ancestors cannot come to us in the form of eagles or peacocks or swans. To obtain something from us, they have to descend from the ancestral dimension in the form of crows alone. Our faraway dear ones have to send the sweet message of their imminent arrival in the harsh tones of the crow.[1] On the other hand, we use the terms 'crow' and 'caw-cawing' in a derogatory way.

My thoughts on the history of crows were disrupted because I suddenly glimpsed a tiny being hiding in the space between the flower pot and the wall. I went closer and saw that it was a tiny baby squirrel that had perhaps fallen out of a nest and was now being sought by the crows as an easy meal.

Two wounds from the beaks of the crow couple had terrified this little life, so he stuck, unmoving, to the flowerpot.

Everyone said that he would not survive the injuries caused by the crows pecking him, so he should be left where he was.

But I couldn't bring myself to leave him there. I gently picked him up and brought him into my room, where I wiped the blood off with a piece of cotton wool and put penicillin ointment on his injuries.

I soaked a thin wick of cotton wool in milk and somehow put it to his tiny mouth, but the mouth would not open, and drops of milk rolled down on both sides.

After several hours of treatment, a drop of water managed to make its way into his mouth. By the third day, he was so reassured and so much better that he held on to my finger with his two small paws and looked around with eyes like blue glass beads.

In three or four months, his silky fur, fluffy tail and mischievously gleaming eyes struck everyone with wonder.

We turned the common noun for his species into a proper noun and began to call him Gillu.[2] I spread some cotton wool in a lightweight basket meant for flowers and suspended it by a cord at the window.

This was Gillu's home for two years. He would rock his home and swing in it while making observations about who knows what inside the room and outside the window with his glass beadlike eyes. Everyone was surprised by his sagacity and his various feats.

Whenever I sat down to write, his desire to attract my attention grew so strong that he devised a good strategy.

He would approach my feet, then ascend the curtain with a whirr and then descend at the same speed. This running up and down would continue until I got up to catch hold of him.

Sometimes, I would put Gillu in a long envelope in such a way that, except for his head and forepaws, all of his slender body was enclosed in the envelope. In this odd situation, he would sometimes stand for hours on the table, propped against the wall, and keep watching my activities with his shiny eyes.

When he grew hungry, he would inform me by chirping, and when he received a cashew or a biscuit, he would remain in the same position, holding it in his forepaws outside the envelope, and keep nibbling at it.

Then came the first springtime of Gillu's life. The fragrance of the *neem-chameli* gently wafted into my room. Squirrels outside the window came up to the screen and said who knows what with their chirps.

Seeing Gillu sitting close to the screen and gazing out at them in a sympathetic manner made me feel that it was necessary to free him.

I removed some nails to open one corner of the screen. Going out by this path, Gillu breathed the air of freedom. Protecting such a small being from domestic dogs and cats inside the house had, in any case, become a problem.

When I go out, my room is kept locked because of the important papers and letters kept in it. When I returned from college and the room was opened, the moment I set foot inside, Gillu would enter through his doorway in the screen and race up and down from my foot to my head and from my head to my foot. This became a daily habit.

When I left the room, he too would go out by the open screen in the window and act as the leader of the squirrel flock, leaping and bounding on every branch, and at exactly four o'clock, he would come in through the window and begin swinging in his swing.

I don't know when or how he developed the desire to startle me. He would hide, sometimes among flowers in the vase, sometimes in the folds of the curtains and sometimes among the leaves of the golden jasmine.

I have many animals and birds who are greatly attached to me, but I don't remember any of them daring to eat from my plate with me.

Gillu was an exception. As soon as I reached the dining room, he would go out of the window, scurry across the yard wall and veranda, reach the table and try to sit in my plate. With great difficulty, I taught him to sit near the plate. Sitting there, he would delicately pick up a grain of rice at a time and neatly consume it. Cashews were his favourite food, and if he didn't get cashews for several days, he would either stop eating other food items or else fling them down from his swing.

Around that time, I was injured in a road accident and had to be hospitalized for some days. During those days, whenever my room was opened, Gillu would jump down from his swing and run up, but as soon as he saw someone else, he would race back to sit in his nest. Everyone who visited gave him cashews, but when I returned from the hospital and cleaned his swing, I found it full of cashews, which

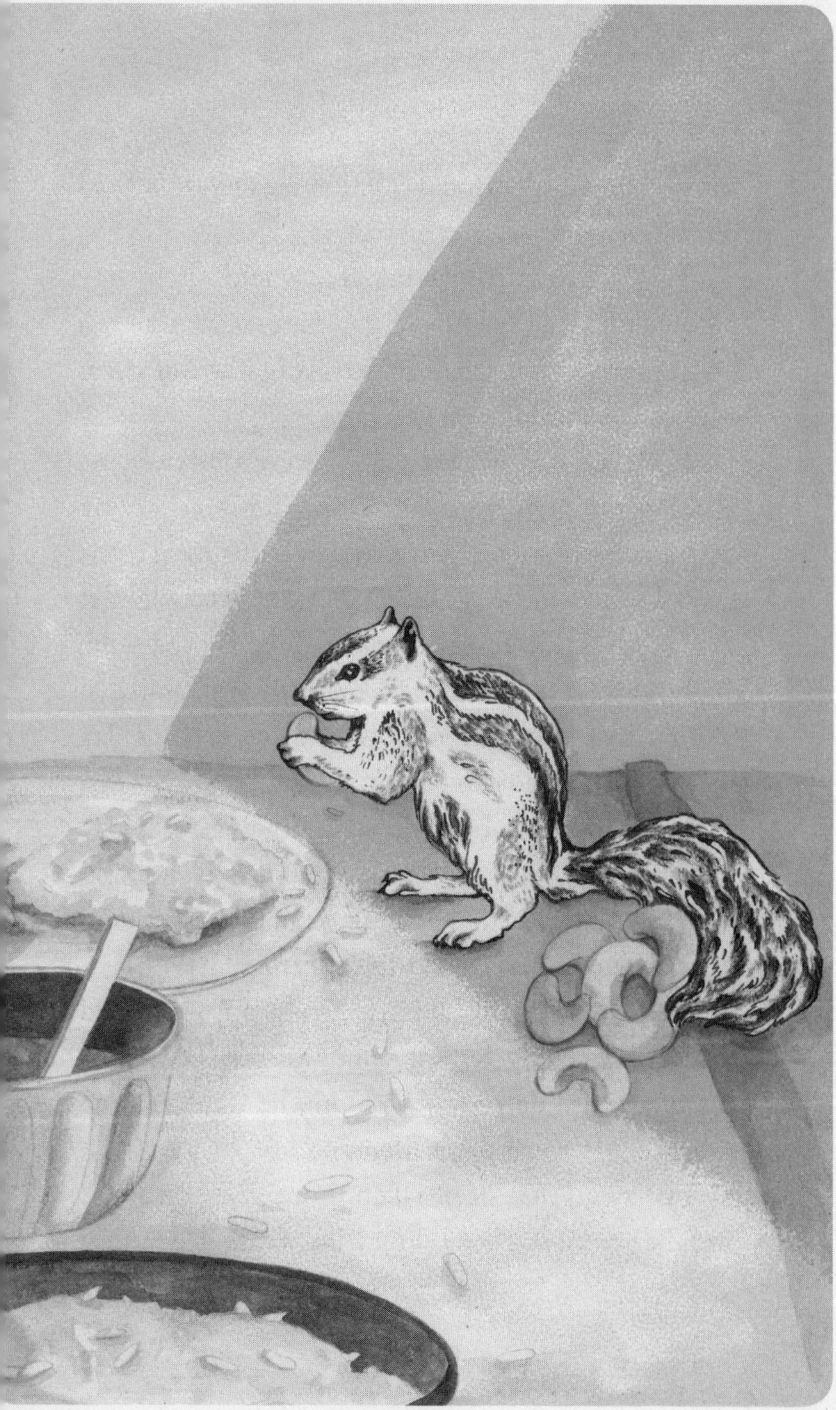

showed how little he had eaten of his favourite food during those days.

While I was recovering, he would sit by my pillow and stroke my head and hair so gently with his tiny paws that when he left, it felt as if a nurse had left.

When I was working on summer afternoons, Gillu would neither go out nor sit in his swing. He devised a way to stay with me and also escape the heat. He would lie down on the clay water goblet near me and thus remain cool as well as close to me.

Squirrels do not live longer than two years, so Gillu's life's journey too drew to its close. One day he neither ate nor went out. At night, in his last agony, he came to bed with me, holding on to my finger, and stayed stuck to my hand, still holding with his cold paws the same finger that he had clung to in infancy when he was near death.

His paws were so cold that I woke up and turned on the heater to give him some warmth. But when the first ray of dawn touched him, he went to sleep to wake into some other life.

His swing has been taken down and put away, and the screen has been closed, but a new generation of squirrels keeps chirping outside the screen, and spring keeps returning to the golden jasmine.

Gillu has been buried beneath the golden jasmine because it was his favourite creeper and also because the belief that his little body will blossom some spring day in a small, yellow jasmine flower continues to console me.

Notes

1. This refers to the Hindu practice of feeding crows on the death anniversaries of ancestors, and the popular belief that a crow cawing in the morning foretells the coming of a guest or a letter.
2. Gillu is an affectionate diminutive of *gilhari*, the Hindi word for squirrel.

Sona the Doe

I am suddenly remembering Sona today because Susmita, granddaughter of my acquaintance, the late Dr Dhirendra Nath Basu, has just written me a note:

> Last year my neighbours gave me a doe. Over the last few months, we have become very fond of her. But I realize that because of her association with deep forests and the fact that she is now full-grown, she needs a larger space to roam about.
>
> Would you be kind enough to accept her? Truly, I will be very grateful because you know that I wouldn't want to give her to someone who

> might mistreat her. I am sure that with you she will be well looked after.

Many years ago, I had decided not to keep a deer again, but now, unless I break my rule it will be impossible to protect this delicate being.

Sona, too, came to me all of a sudden, but she was an infant. Her small, tender body was like a knot of golden silk tassels. A little face and large watery eyes. When she looked at you, it seemed as if tears were about to spill out of those eyes. A sleeping wave of lightning in them dazzled one.

Everyone was so impressed by her simple, infant being that names like Sona, Suvarna, Suvarnarekha, appropriate to a golden-magnolia-complexioned beauty, became her epithets.

But the story of that poor baby doe is one of those sorrowful stories of earth that are written by human cruelty. It is not the story of a priceless diamond from an inaccessible mine or a valuable pearl from the fathomless ocean.

Humans ornament their bodies with lifeless things. There is no story to be told about these things except a change in their condition. But the kind of living nourishment humans want for their bodies or their egos creates a survival struggle which is the essence of all living beings' story.

Only those who have seen a herd of deer leaping along on a plain surging with greenery can imagine that marvellous, mobile beauty. It is like the turbulence of waves topped with golden foam in an ocean of liquid emeralds. But a hunter is not enchanted by this ever-moving loveliness of life.

I often wonder how a person can term it a sport to render this vital energy inactive and inanimate.

Humans consider death not only ugly but impure. The corpses of even those dearest to one are felt to be impure, untouchable and fearful. If death is so impure and ugly, I do not understand why it is not thought impure and ugly to go around spreading death.

How beautiful birds are, flying in the sky like clouds of multicoloured flowers and playing an orchestra of veena, flute, drum and *jal-tarang*.[1] A human picks up a gun, takes aim, and several singing and flying birds fall to the ground like so many pebbles. The neck of a red-and-yellow-beaked one is broken, the beautiful yellow claws of another are rendered crooked, and the rainbow-like feathers of another lie scattered. Neither beauty nor music remains in those tattered, blood-soaked, dead and half-dead little leaves, yet the killer dances with pleasure at his success.

The human play of destruction is just as cruel in the world of animals as in the world of birds. No animal is as beautiful and meek as the deer—its eyes are hieroglyphics of gentleness. But even its mobile, living beauty is unable to please the human heart. Humans are the highest form of life—why are they so indifferent and averse to other forms of life and so attracted and enthralled by death?

It was humans' cruel love of the sport that brought poor Sona away from her forest home and her own tribe to live in human society.

When a herd of deer indolently ruminating in the peaceful woodland was startled and ran at the sound of the hunters' approach, Sona's mother, having just given birth, was unable to flee. The newborn baby deer could not run, so the mother doe gave up her life trying to protect her child with her own body.

Inspired either by pity or by the love of a new spectacle, the hunters picked up the live baby clinging to the dead deer's blood-soaked and cold udders. The wife and children of one of them kept the baby alive for a few days by feeding it milk mixed with water.

A girl thought of me, just as Susmita Basu has, and she brought the orphaned baby in a near-dead condition to me. The baby was unwanted, and there was not much hope of her survival, but I accepted her. Everyone started calling her Sona because of her silky golden colour. After collecting a milk bottle, glucose, goat's milk and so on, the difficult enterprise of raising her began.

Her mouth was so small that the nipple of the bottle would not fit into it. Also, she did not know how to drink. Gradually, she learnt not only to drink but also to recognize the bottle. While she was frolicking and gambolling in the courtyard, she would notice Bhaktin washing the bottle and would come running up to look at it with her liquid, amazed eyes as if it were a living friend.[2]

She had learnt to snuggle up to the leg of my bed at night, but it took her some days to develop the habit of not defecating there. As soon as darkness fell, she would come and sit near my bed and would leave the room only at daybreak.

Her daily routine was pretty regular. At first, she was a curiosity for the girl students in the school and the hostel, but after some days, she became so dear a companion to them that they couldn't enjoy any activity without her.

After drinking milk and eating soaked chickpeas, Sona would steady her four legs and go bounding around the compound. Then she would go to the hostel and examine the interior and exterior of every room. The hostel is variously active in the morning—one girl washes her hands and face, another combs her hair, one changes her sari, another cleans her desk, one bathes and spreads out her wet clothes to dry while another does her puja. When Sona appeared, new elements were added to this varied congestion of activities. One student would make a large mark on Sona's forehead with vermilion, another would tie a ribbon around her neck, and a third would feed her sweets offered in the puja.

When she arrived at the mess, not only the girls but the servants too would run up, eager to feed her something or other, but except for biscuits, she didn't much care for human food.

When the chapter of awakening the hostel and breakfasting there closed, she would arrive on the lawn to graze and to roll on the grass. I am not sure how she figured out my breakfast time, but she would come in exactly at that time and stand close to me until I finished eating. A share of the rice and roti was her due, but she liked raw vegetables best.

As soon as the bell rang, she would adjourn to the assembly ground for prayers. After that, she would begin going in and out of classrooms just as she went in and out of hostel rooms in the morning.

She preferred the younger children because they had more time to play with her. They would stand in a row, calling, 'Sona, Sona,' and she would leap over them one by one till she reached the end of the line, then do the same on the way back. This circus-like game could go on for hours as one class after another kept coming out for playtime.

She had many ways of expressing affection for me. When I stood outside, she would leap over my head from either the front or the back. Onlookers would usually get frightened, thinking that her hooves would injure my head, but she would tuck up her legs in such a manner and leap so high that there was no question of my getting hurt.

When I came inside, she would rub against my legs, when I sat down, she would take the end of my sari into her mouth, and sometimes she would stand silently behind me and chew my plaited hair. When I scolded her, she would look fixedly at me with such inexpressible curiosity in her big, round, wondering eyes that I couldn't help laughing.

Only when one raises a deer does one understand why Kalidasa, the teacher of all poets, gives deer, does and fawns such importance in his plays.

When you raise a deer, it is no longer an animal but an affectionate companion who fills the empty spaces of your loneliness but never burdens you with irritating inquisitiveness. If humans communicated only with their eyes, many arguments would come to an end, but nature must have thought this undesirable.

Perhaps it is because of this that one's spirit, wounded by human voices attacking one another and by the burden of meaningful words, longs to be healed and consoled by the sandal paste of these wordless beings' fluid, affectionate gaze.

In sage Kanva's hermitage, resonant with the voice of Saraswati, the presence of dumb, unknowing deer was indispensable along with the sages, sages' wives and hermit boys and girls. Deer surround the cottages purified by mantras, seeking to block their doorways. As Shakuntala bids farewell, the young fawn she has raised like a son catches hold of her sari end, in which she has gathered so many blessings and so much advice from her elders. When Shakuntala asks who is pulling her sari, Kanva replies:

yasya tvaya vranaviropanamigudinaam
tailam nyashichyata mukhe kushasuchibiddha
shyaamaakamushti parivardhitako jahaati
soyam na putrakritakaha padavim mrigaste[3]

He whose mouth you heal with wild almond oil
when it gets cut by salt reed-grass,
he whom you have raised, feeding him fistfuls of
barnyard millet,
he who is like a son to you,
that deer of yours is stopping you.[4]

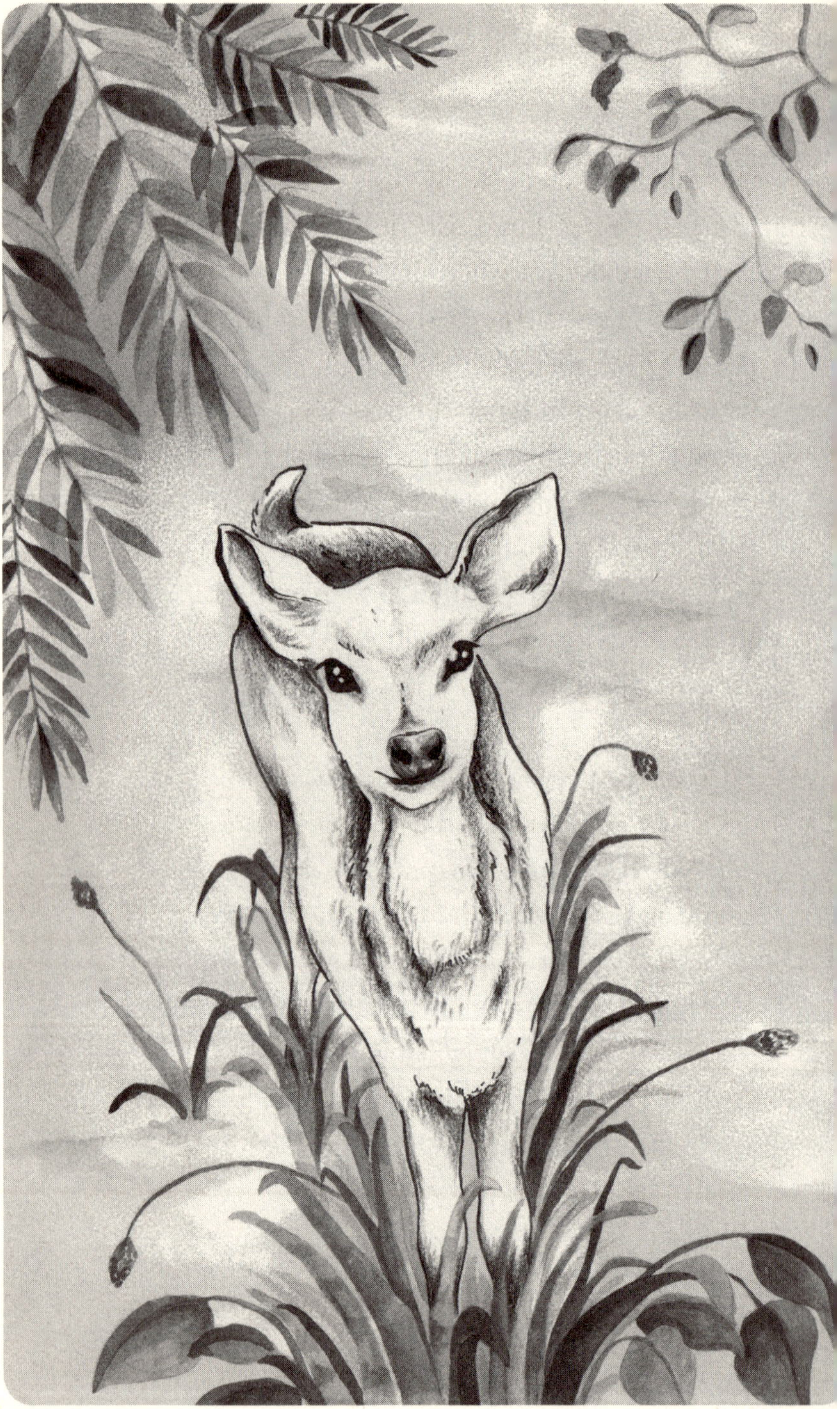

Deer have an especially heart-touching role not only in literature but in folk songs too.

Animals recognize humans' unpretentious affection but not high and low social status. I absorbed this truth from Sona by osmosis.

What had Sona to do with the grave and solemn Guru-ji of the girl students? She knew that look which conveyed affection for her and those hands which had untiringly held the milk bottle to her mouth.

If Sona felt it necessary to jump over my head to express her affection, she would do so. It was impossible for her to be impressed by my status or circumstances.

A dog knows the difference between the master of the house and workers in the house and is aware of the master's every mood, whether affectionate or angry. When lovingly called, a dog gladly comes close, and when anger is expressed, he cowers pitifully in fear.

But a deer does not know this difference, so it is hard for her to fear the one who has raised her. If one gets angry with her, she stands there, her eyes meeting the eyes of the one who raised her.

Those alarmed-looking eyes of hers look even more astonished than usual. As if she asks, 'Is this right?' A deer recognizes affection alone and makes special efforts to show acceptance of it.

My cat Godhuli, dogs Hemant and Basant and bitch Flora were annoyed when this new guest arrived, but Sona became friends with all of them in a few days. She would lie down on the grass, and the dogs and cat would leap and gambol around her. One would pull her ear, another her foot and once they were all immersed in the game, she would suddenly go bounding off, and they would scamper after her.

After a year, Sona began to change from a fawn to a doe. The yellowish hair on her body began to glow with a coppery hue. Her legs grew rounded, and her black hooves became shiny. Her neck grew more curved and supple. The ripples on her back began to gleam. But her most remarkable features were visible in her eyes, her way of looking. Her blue eyes framed by collyrium-like black lines looked as if electricity were bursting from sapphire bulbs.

Perhaps a memory world of the forest and her own community was awakening within her. Often, in the empty playground, she would stand with her head held high as if waiting to hear someone coming. When spring breezes began to blow, this silent waiting touched something in her. She was no longer as entertained as she used to be by the frolicking of her childhood companions, so her moments of waiting grew longer.

At this time, Flora had four puppies in a hidden corner of Bhaktin's dark storeroom, and forgetting her playmates, she busied herself with this new creation of hers. Sona spent only one day searching for her female friend, then seeing her surrounded by so many small beings, her look, which was naturally that of wonder, grew gravely amazed.

One day I saw that Flora had gone roaming outside, and Sona was lying, relaxed, in Bhaktin's storeroom. The puppies, who were still blind, were whimpering and seeking milk in Sona's udders. After that, lying down among the puppies became part of Sona's daily routine. Surprisingly, Flora, who never allowed Hemant, Basant or Godhuli to go anywhere near her children, would leave them in Sona's protection and wander off on her own quite contentedly.

She had probably understood Sona's affectionate and non-violent nature. When the puppies grew bigger, and their eyes opened, Sona incorporated them into the army that followed her around, and as if celebrating this expansion, she spent more time than usual leaping back and forth over my head. But after some days, when this festivity palled, her motionless times of silent, wordless waiting returned.

That summer, I was to journey to Badrinath. Because of the animals I have fostered, I usually don't travel much. Even though there are workers to look after them, I feel somewhat uncomfortable leaving them. Bhaktin, Anurup and others were going along with me. I decided to take Flora along as well because she could not stay without me.

The hostel was closed, so Sona's usual activities were at a standstill. In my absence, she had little to give her pleasure or delight.

Hemant and Basant were used to my travelling and absence. As soon as the holdall was spread out and the bedding placed in it, they would run and lie down on it and begin to reproach me with their barking and whining. If they were not tied up, they would get into the car and sit down or else run behind it all the way to the station. But once I was gone, they would wait sadly for my return.

No idea of such an eventuality as my travelling or my return had made its way into Sona's consciousness, so I could easily imagine her despair, her confusion, and her perplexity.

Because I had decided to make the pilgrimage on foot, the Badrinath journey took up the whole summer vacation. When I returned on the second of July and stood at the door of the bungalow, a tumult broke out among those I had reared and from whom I had been separated.

Godhuli leapt up on to my shoulder. Hemant and Basant ran around me repeatedly, barking in welcome, but my eyes were searching for Sona. Why was she not here, leaping over my head to show her joy? When I asked where Sona was, the gardener began to wipe his eyes while the peon and watchman looked away from me and at one another. They didn't want to give me sad news the moment I arrived, but the gardener's emotion gave me that news without words.

I found out that the silence in the hostel and Flora's and my absence made Sona so insecure that she would wander around, searching, and would often go out of the compound, intent on this search. Not many people would want to adopt such a big doe, but many would desire to obtain her flesh and enjoy its taste. For fear of this, the gardener began to tie her in the playground with a long rope.

One day, who knows in what oppressive state she forgot the boundaries of her bondage and leapt so high that the rope brought her crashing to earth. That was her last breath and her last leap.

All of them went together to put her body, which was like a bundle of golden silk, into the Ganga and thus ended the sad story of Sona who was born in a forest and raised in a close-knit community.

Hearing this, I decided that I would not keep a deer again, but things have turned out in such a way that I now have to do so.

Notes

1. The jal-tarang is an Indian percussion instrument, first mentioned in the fourth-century Kamasutra. It consists of bowls filled with water, which are played by striking the edges with two small sticks.

2. Bhaktin was Mahadevi's housekeeper. Mahadevi's pen portrait of her appears in *Smriti ki Rekhayen* (Lines of Memory).
3. From Kalidasa's play *Abhijnanashakuntalam*.
4. Kanva is a sage who adopted Shakuntala as a baby, just as she adopts the deer, so there is a special tenderness to this description.

Durmukh the Rabbit

No one will believe that the one who was termed quarrelsome in everyday language, and Durmukh (foul-mouthed) or Durvasa (one difficult to live with) in pure Sanskrit, was a tender-limbed rabbit. Sometimes reality outpaces imagination.

The gardener named him Laraku because he refused to consort with any other animal of his own or another tribe. My girl students began to call him Durmukh because of his readiness to bite, and I bestowed on him the epithet Durvasa because of his inexplicably wrathful temperament.

One need not apologize for the name Laraku, but the misuse of legendary names like Durmukh and Durvasa is definitely a cause for concern.[1]

I, too, am displeased with Durmukh. He worked as a secret agent for Ram, the ideal man. He told Ram about the washerman's slander of Sita, which led to Sita's banishment. A king employs secret agents to procure information about enemy kings, not to find out about private conversations between couples in every home. Everyone knows that husbands and wives say all kinds of things to one another in anger. When the anger dies down, they say, 'Oh, forget about it, who knows what I said in a temper,' and thus apologize to each other. Every householder is the king of his house and his wife queen. A secret agent, even a royal one, goes beyond the bounds of duty and behaves wickedly when he reports their private conversations as public events.

It is clear from this that by naming the rabbit, who was adept at misusing his sharp teeth, Durmukh, we did not insult Ram's wicked secret agent. But for making such daring use of the great sage Durvasa's name, I had to regularly beg forgiveness of his fearsome memory. There is no way to know whether that great sage, having achieved liberation, is now creating waves of anger in the formless supreme self or is terrifying the inhabitants of some other world with his curses. Perhaps, having discovered by his inner vision that this rabbit's angry temperament could express itself only because it was named after him, he had forgiven me; otherwise, my audacity would not have remained uncursed thus far.

The way I obtained that rabbit Durvasa can only be called an unfortunate chance. A nice couple, who were my neighbours, had raised a pair of rabbits in a burrow in their backyard. Every evening, the housewife put a small basket over the entrance to the tunnel and weighted it down with a flat stone. One night, she forgot to secure the entrance to the burrow, and a cat who was always on the lookout for such an opportunity made her way in and tore to pieces the two rabbits and three of their children. Only one baby rabbit, who was hidden under his mother's feet, survived.

The gardener solved the problem of rearing this tiny life by bringing it to my house. Rabbits are mammals so we tried to rear him by feeding him milk with a cotton wick. He lived in my room. A fluffy cushion was placed on a cane-topped stool as a seat and bed for him, but he usually fell asleep next to my pillow. As he grew, though, his wrathful temperament began to cause dismay and consternation.

Rabbits are meek and timid. They have teeth but do not bite, claws but do not scratch. Fear is their dominant emotion. The new resident rabbit entirely disproved all our notions. If his meal of rice and milk was delayed, he would overturn his dish with his paws, he would sink his sharp teeth into the giver's hand or else foot if the hand were out of reach, and he would race round the room throwing and overturning whatever he found. For fear of him, not only lizards but insects and moths too stayed away from my room.

He was nice-looking like other rabbits, with one distinguishing feature. His body was covered with thick, soft and shining fur; his tail was small and pretty. He constantly cleaned his face with his neat little paws. His ears were shorter than those of foreign breeds, but there was an especially alluring beauty in their shapeliness and their way of standing upright. His unique feature was that he had one black ear and one white ear. The eye near his black ear was black and the eye near his white ear was red.

Typically, white rabbits have red eyes and black or dappled ones have black eyes. But this rabbit's eyes, with their two differing colours, were an exception to the rule. Sometimes it seemed as if the halves of two different rabbits had been joined together to make one, and a sparkling sapphire and ruby had been implanted in its eyes. He completely lacked his community's alertness and apprehensive body language.

My room has screen netting doors on springs, and the windows too have screens. No cat or dog could come in all of a sudden, but they would often stand outside the screen and wait for me. The rabbit would not run away or try to hide but instead would go right up to the screen and stand there in a rage, glaring at them with his red and black eyes. Durmukh's presence in my room had resulted in the banishment of all the other animals and birds, so once he became somewhat bigger, sturdier, and smoother, I thought it best for him to be transferred to the aviary. Half of the floor there was cement and the other half mud because animals like rabbits are happy only when they can dig the earth and make dwellings for themselves. Their natural development and enjoyment of life are obstructed in a cage or a house with a concrete floor.

Durmukh first dug the earth and made a tunnel-like home for himself, and as soon as he had completed this construction project, he declared war on all the other inhabitants of the aviary. His pouncing and biting made it difficult for the pigeons and peacocks to descend to the ground for grain. They would keep sitting on their perches and swings until Durmukh had eaten his fill and withdrawn to his burrow to rest. Sometimes, even from his burrow, he would hear his rivals descending and would suddenly mount an assault, digging his sharp teeth into the neck of one and the feet of another until they flew up, crying out in pain.

Finally, thinking that Durmukh's wrathful temperament might be due to loneliness and longing for another member of his own community, I bought a rabbit bride from Bade Miyan of Nakkhas Kona. She gleamed white as snow, and her eyes were beautiful like red coral, so we named her Himani. But my notion that Durmukh would behave like a courteous rabbit with her turned

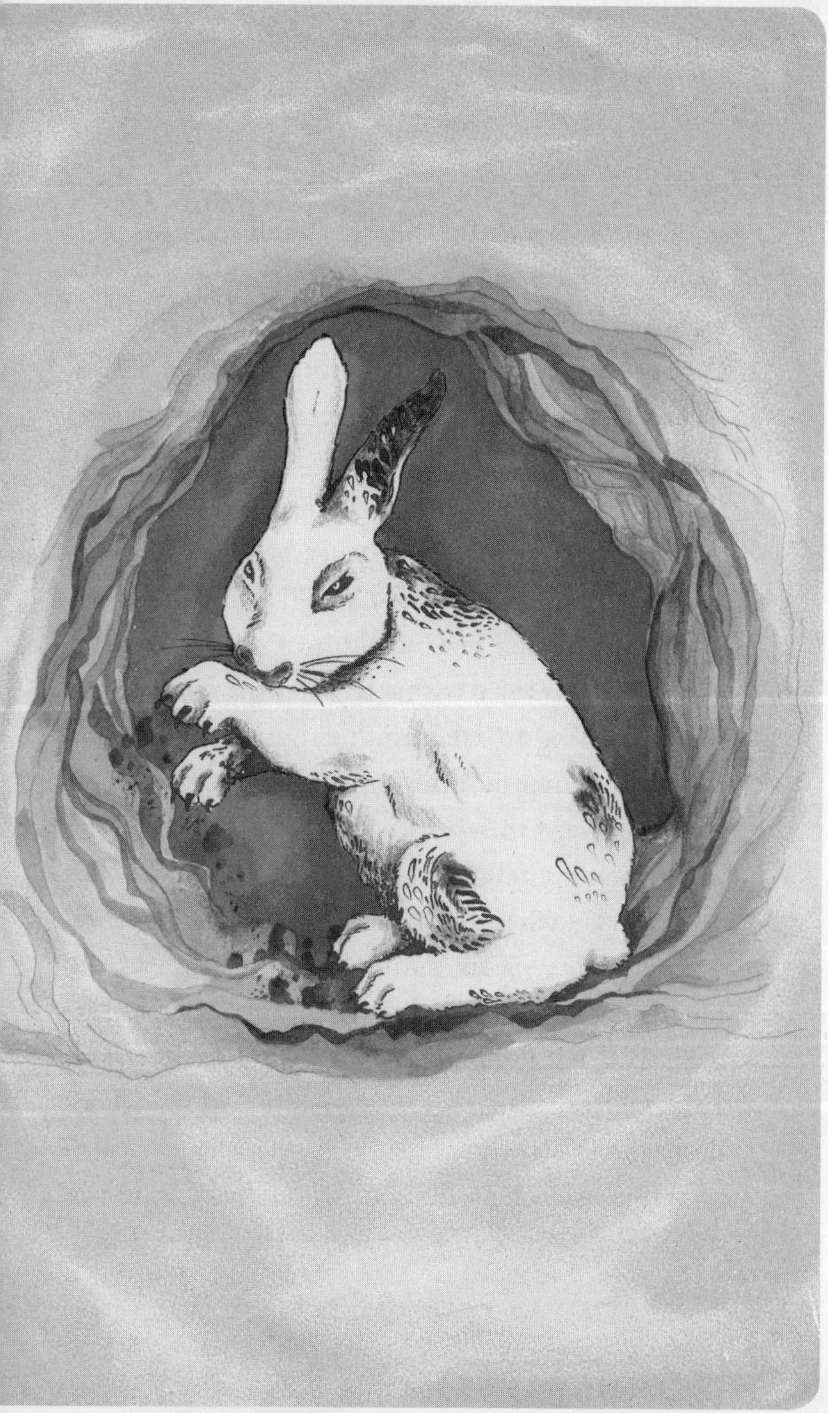

out to be quite unfounded. He cast a fiery look at the newcomer from his black and red eyes as if mingling smoke and flame and then attacked. We had great difficulty in protecting the poor thing. Durmukh would not let her near his burrow. Once, when Himani took advantage of his absence to dare enter his mansion, the master of the burrow returned suddenly, and not only did he drag her out by the ears but also bit her beautiful, tender, snowy ears until they were covered in blood. When poor Himani dug her own burrow and prepared a bedroom by lining it with soft green grass, Durmukh began fighting to establish his right over that too. After the winter months passed and the longer days of spring warmth returned, we saw a slight change in Durmukh's delight in warfare.

One day when Himani issued from her burrow with an army of six bunny babies, a wave of joy ran through not only the aviary but my house as well. But with the coming of this new creation, Durmukh's causeless fury too returned in all its destructive intensity.

He would chew the foot of one baby, bite the ear of another and wound the back of a third.

Those babies, tender as the fluffy, ball-like flowers of the *kadamba* tree, would be speckled red with blood. Himani, too, would constantly get injured in her attempts to protect her offspring. The aviary under the Ashoka tree, shaded by the *quisqualis* creeper,[2] reeked of Loraxin ointment, Nebasulf powder and cotton wool, reminding one of a hospital.

Then one day, Durmukh flew into a rage and wounded the tender necks of two bunny babies so severely with his sharp teeth that their lives could not be saved. When the situation waxed so grave, I decided to isolate him. A small wire house was made next to the big wire house and Durmukh was transferred into it. From there, he could see everyone else but was not able to attack them. In the first few days of his banishment, he kept raging in futile fury. Then he busied himself in digging a burrow. He had come up with an ingenious plan, beyond our imagination, for getting into the big wire house. He dug a long tunnel in the ground, which reached the big wire house, and began to come and go as he pleased. The gardener used a stone to close the mouth of the tunnel that issued into the big wire house, but it was difficult to stop Durmukh's invasions. He kept digging new entryways from the tunnel and launching surprise assaults, turning the aviary into a battlefield. His children grew up and had children of their own, but none of them proved capable of confronting and defeating Durmukh or winning his heart by filial affection. Had death not defeated him, this process would have gone on forever.

Then one day, we found Durmukh lying cold and unmoving, with a young snake's tail crushed between his teeth. The snake's head was under his paws.

The smell of rabbits usually attracts snakes because rabbits are among their favourite foods. Perhaps this baby snake had entered through the netting, attracted by the smell, because it was difficult for a full-grown snake to do so. Durmukh must have pounced on it as was his wont. He could have climbed up on the platform within his wire house, where a snake could not reach or he could have gone through his tunnel to the big wire house where the stopped-up drain would have prevented the snake from entering, but his ever-aggressive nature would not permit him to accept defeat or escape. Even a wrathful nature, in its terrestrial form, lacks the poisonous power to kill, so poor Durmukh could not withstand the young snake's poisonous bite, but before he died, he took his revenge by cutting his foe in half.

We built him a tomb in the big aviary. Few know that all of my hundred or so rabbits are descendants of Durmukh. His posterity does not have the ability to grasp his history, but his characteristics are often discussed in my house.

Even today, my gardener is convinced that that rabbit was possessed by the spirit of a wrestler, a pahalwan-ji, for how else could a rabbit possibly fight a snake and cut it in half? There is a samadhi of a pahalwan somewhere nearby, and his powers are so renowned that villagers come from near and far to pray for boons there.

But I still remember that tiny white bunny baby, tender as a magnolia flower, whose life at its very inception unfortunately came under the cruel shadow of a cat. Had he grown up like other rabbits, eating and playing under his mother's affectionate shadow, who knows how he would have turned out?

Notes

1. Laraku means 'quarrelsome'. In the Ramayana, there is a demon named Durmukh. But the author here has in mind Bhavabhuti's Sanskrit play *Uttararamacharit*, in which Durmukh is Rama's spy who brings him the information that some of his subjects criticize him for accepting Sita even though she had spent time in Ravana's palace. Durvasa was a famously irascible sage, who cursed many, such as Indra and Shakuntala, but also granted boons, for example, to Kunti in the Mahabharata.
2. Malti or Rangoon creeper, Latin name *quisqualis*, which means 'what is this?'.

Gaura the Cow

Gaura was the adolescent calf of a cow raised in my sister's home. She had been reared with such tender care that she was somewhat different from other calves.

One day, my sister said, 'You have so many animals and birds—why don't you keep a cow who will be useful?' My younger sister, Shyama, is much older than me in worldly wisdom and since childhood has always been highly praised for her efficiency and practical skills.

When she makes a confident statement, her opinion, like a contagious illness, immediately influences the listener. It was not surprising, therefore, that her lecture on utilitarianism impacted me so greatly that it immediately became necessary to implement her suggestion.

I have never liked to keep animals or birds to solve a food-related problem. My mind revolts as soon as I think of the main purpose for which goats, chickens and fish are raised.

But that day, I looked closely at Gaura. Strong, curved legs, full haunches, a smooth, plump back, a long, well-shaped neck, small horns beginning to sprout, ears like two half-opened lotuses suggesting the redness within, a long tail ending in a thick black tuft reminiscent of a fly-whisk—everything was well shaped as if in a mould. As if a cow had been sculpted of Italian marble and polished to perfection.

There is a special gleam in the whiteness of a healthy animal's pores. Gaura's radiance was such that it seemed as if every fibre had been rubbed with powdered mica so that wherever the light fell on her, it gave rise to a special glow.

As soon as I saw Gaura, my dilemma about whether to raise a cow changed into a resolution.

When the cow reached my bungalow, a wave of reverence arose among my acquaintances and workers. She was garlanded with red and white roses, a big tika of saffron and vermilion was applied to her forehead, she was worshipped with a four-wicked lamp and fed with sweets made of curds. She was named Gaurangini and called Gaura for short.[1] I don't know how this adoration affected her, but she certainly seemed very pleased. The flame of the *arati* lamp shimmering and blossoming in her big, black, shining eyes produced the illusion of many lamps. As if someone had set several lamps afloat on a wave that looked black by night.

Gaura was indeed lovely to look at. The liquid beauty of her crystalline black eyes, in particular, held and steadied one's vision. On her long, shapely face and broad, bright brow, her eyes were like pools of blue water in ice. There was a uniquely confident expression in her eyes. Unlike the stricken, astonished look in a deer's eyes, a cow's eyes look self-confident. This animal is not only tortured but cruelly killed by humans, yet terror and amazement do not replace the confidence in her eyes.

Only by looking into her eyes can one understand why Mahatma Gandhi said that 'the cow is a poem of pity'.

Few comparisons can be found for Gaura's slow, languorous walk. There is beauty in speed, but not as much beauty as in a slow pace. The speed of an arrow can dazzle the eyes for a moment but a flower's slow, circular movement in a gentle breeze is a feast for the eyes.

In a few days she became so intimate with everyone that the other animals and birds forgot their own smallness and her largeness. The cats and dogs played under her belly and between her legs. The birds perched on her back and forehead and tickled her ears and eyes. She would stand still with closed eyes, as if lost in the pleasure of this contact.

She began to recognize us all, not only by our voices but even by our footsteps. She had such an accurate sense of time that she would start mooing to call me as soon as the car entered the gate. She knew my times for tea, snacks and meals so well that after waiting for a little while to get her share, she would make the house resound with her bellows.

Her companionable attachment to me needed closeness just as human affection does. When I went near her, she would stretch out her neck to be stroked, and on being patted, she would confidingly put her face on my shoulder and close her eyes. When I walked away, she would keep turning her neck to look after me. She could make only one sound to express her needs. But shades of joy, sorrow, indifference, yearning and other emotions swam in her big, black eyes.

After a year, Gaura became the mother of a beautiful, healthy son. Because of his ruddy colour, the calf looked like an image made of red clay. He had a white mark on his forehead shaped like a betel leaf and white rings around his legs just above the hooves so that it seemed as if a red clay image of a calf had been decked with silver ornaments. The calf was named Lalmani, but everyone called him Lalu.[2] When mother and son were together, they reminded one of snow and fire. Now a veritable milk festival began in our house. Gaura usually gave about twelve *ser* milk,[3] so even after leaving plenty for Lalmani, there was enough milk to make the blessing 'may you bathe in milk' come true for all the baby Krishnas of the neighbourhood as well as for all the dogs and cats.[4] The dogs and cats created a strange scenario. They would sit in a line in front of Gaura at milking time, and Mahadev would put out each one's dish. With perfect politeness, they would wait like guests invited for a special occasion. Milk would be measured out in each dish, and after drinking it, they would leap and gambol around Gaura, expressing gratitude each in his or her own way. Until they left, Gaura would observe them all, as if highly pleased. On days when their arrival was delayed, she would keep mooing as if calling out to them.

But now, the problem of milking her needed a permanent resolution. The workers who were urban didn't know how to milk, and those who hailed from villages were so out of practice that it took them hours to finish milking. When the milkman who used to deliver milk before Gaura started giving milk requested to be appointed for this task, we found a solution to the problem.

After two or three months, Gaura's food intake dropped sharply, and she kept growing weaker and less active. I was worried and called in veterinarians. They kept trying various investigations, tests, X-rays in order to arrive at a diagnosis. Finally, they decided that someone had fed the cow a needle, which was being carried to her heart in her bloodstream.

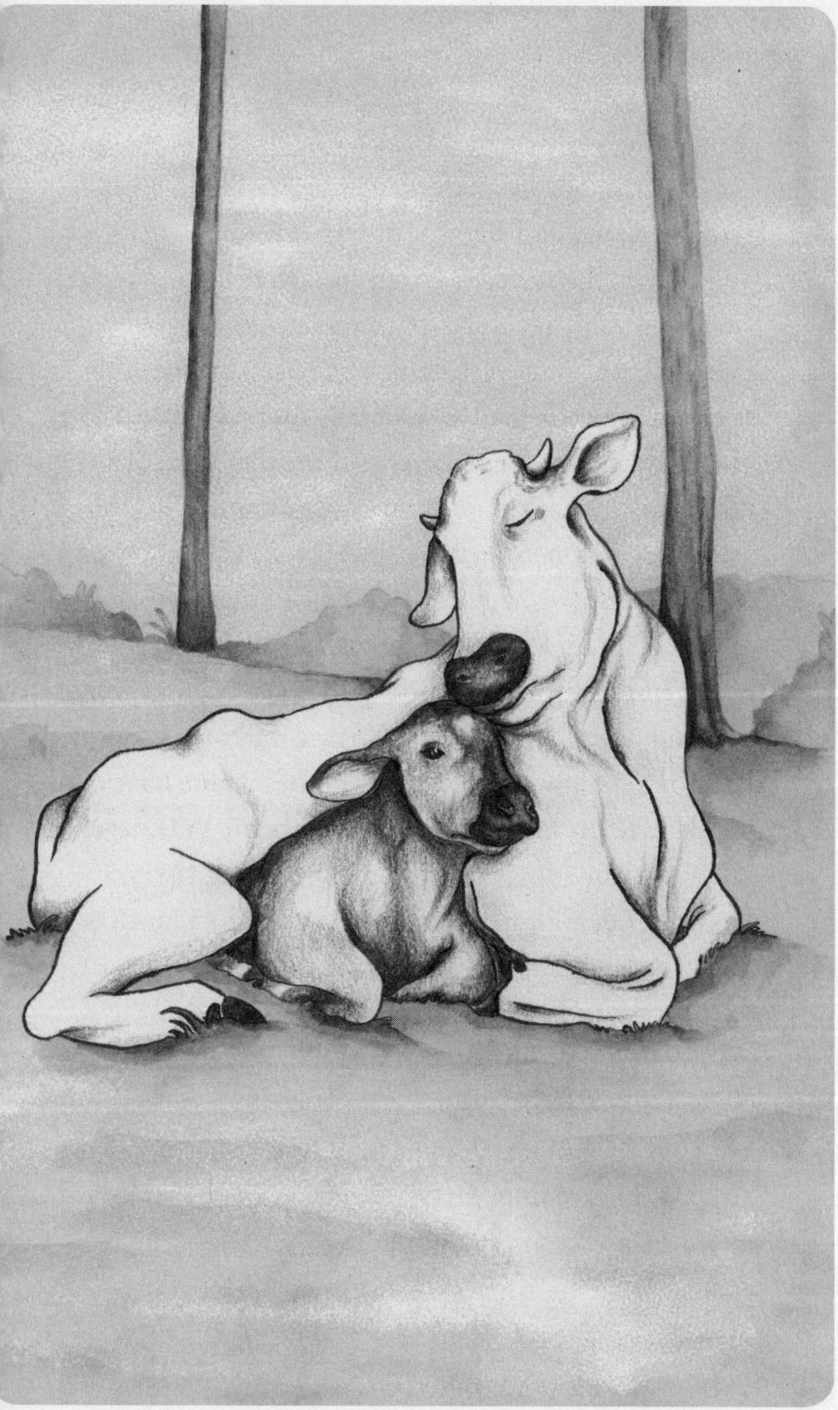

When the needle pierced her heart, blood would stop flowing, and she would certainly die.

I was distressed as well as astonished. What could be the meaning of someone feeding her a needle? We, ourselves, took care of feeding her, but perhaps a needle had accidentally found its way into her fodder. But the doctors told me that a needle in the fodder would stick in the cow's mouth. The only way to get a needle down her throat and into her bloodstream to her heart would be to deliberately insert it into a large lump of raw sugar.

The cruel truth that finally emerged was one that I could never have imagined. Some milkmen cannot bear the coming of a cow into homes where a lot of milk used to be purchased from them. Whenever they find an opportunity, they bring about the cow's untimely death by feeding her a needle in a lump of raw sugar. After the cow dies, they once again start delivering milk to those homes. As soon as we got to know about the needle, the milkman vanished, so it was natural for suspicion to become a certainty. Even if he had not disappeared, it would have been impossible to find the necessary evidence to take legal measures against him.

Then began Gaura's struggle with death, the memory of which still makes my heart shudder. The doctors said that feeding a cow apple juice might result in calcium forming around the needle, preventing it from piercing the heart, so we regularly extracted juice from several ser of apples and fed it to Gaura through a tube. She was given injections to strengthen her. Animals have to be given injections with a long, thick needle that is like a gimlet and a large bottle of medicine, so the injections in themselves were like torturous surgeries. But Gaura quietly endured both the external and internal piercing and pain. Only sometimes two drops would fall from the corners of her large but sad eyes.

She could not stand up now but when I drew near, a shadow of happiness seemed to swim in her eyes. When I sat by her, she would put her head on my shoulder and lick my neck with her rough tongue.

Poor Lalmani had no idea of his mother's illness and imminent death. He was given another cow's milk, which he did not enjoy. He wanted to drink his mother's milk and play with her, so whenever he got a chance he would go to Gaura and either butt her repeatedly to make her get up or else keep leaping and running around her.

I have kept many living creatures, so I have had to bid a timely or untimely farewell to some of them. But I don't remember a more piercing sorrow than this one.

That such a healthy, beautiful cow, radiant as milk, giver of milk, would become lifeless and unmoving any moment now, leaving behind her lovely, playful calf—the thought brought me to tears.

I summoned veterinarians from Lucknow, Kanpur and other cities, and the local veterinarians visited two or three times a day, but no one could come up with a treatment that would give us a ray of hope. Only one who has sat beside a patient suffering from an incurable and fatal illness knows the anguish of waiting for inexorable death.

When Gaura's beautiful, shining eyes lost their light and even apple juice would not go down her throat, I knew that the end was near. Now I had just one wish—to be with her at the end. Day and night, I would get up many times to go and see her.

One day, I went to see her at four in the morning during the *brahma muhurta*, and as always, she put her head on my shoulder.[5] Suddenly, it grew heavy as stone, slid down my arm and came to rest on the earth. Perhaps the needle had pierced her heart and stopped it.

I have always given to the Ganga the mortal remains of the living beings I have reared. When we took Gaurangini, an ocean of tenderness and pathos surged up, but Lalmani thought this too was a game and continued his gambolling. If a deep sigh could be translated into words, its echo would say, 'Alas, my cow-protecting country!'

Notes

1. Gaurangini means 'fair-limbed' and is one of the names of Goddess Parvati as is the diminutive Gaura, which means 'fair' or 'beautiful'.
2. Lalmani means 'red jewel'.
3. Close to ten kilogrammes.
4. Children are often identified with the child Krishna, hence this means that after the calf had drunk, there was enough milk for all the small children in the neighbourhood as well as for the dogs and cats in Mahadevi's household.

'May you bathe in milk' is a common blessing, suggesting abundance.

5. 'Brahma muhurta', literally, the auspicious time of Brahma, the Creator God. It refers to the time before sunrise, which is considered the best time for meditation.

Neelu the Dog

Neelu's story is inseparable from that of his mother, so if one story is told without the other, it remains incomplete.

His Alsatian mother lived in a Himalayan village and was called Lucy. Her body was moulded to run like a deer, like the wind, and had not an ounce of extra flesh. Her brownish-yellowish fur that appeared black, her small black eyes radiating intelligence, her alert ears standing upright and her long thick, furry tail touching her ankles all contributed to her regal appearance. And she truly was different from other dogs.

Alsatian dogs accept only one master. If, due to circumstances, they do not have one person as master, they treat everyone as companions. This means that they do not obey anyone's orders but are ready to oblige anyone who shows them affection. Lucy, too, behaved like a free companion to everyone.

From her village, a narrow field path led through two mountains down to the tarred road at the end of which was just one grocery store at the motor stop. In winter, the gap between the two mountain walls filled up with snow and no sign of a path remained. Then the villagers, unable to reach the shop, would tie to Lucy's neck a large towel or sheet containing some money and a list of items, and would request her to bring the stuff for them. With the intuitive knowledge of how to make a path through the snow that she had inherited from her lineage, she would traverse all obstacles and reach the shop. The shopkeeper would take the cloth and money from her neck, read the list, and tie a bundle of goods to her neck or back, and Lucy, carrying that burden, would return along the icy path.

There were days when she had to make the journey several times. Someone would remember to send for sugar but forget to ask for tea, remember the flour but forget the potatoes. Lucy never complained of the customers' forgetfulness. As soon as the cloth was tied to her neck, she would depart like an arrow. Because of her ready willingness, the customers' tendency to forget escalated. One day, a mountain dog, wandering through the snow, came to the shop from a village somewhere higher up, and Lucy made friends with him. The two looked as different as a finely carved statue and an unshapen rock, but having shared dark days, they became companions.

That winter, Lucy extended her lineage by giving birth to two pups, but one died of cold, and the other began to struggle with the bone-chilling environment on the strength of his vital heat alone.

In the winter, hyenas often come down from the higher mountains and are found roaming around in the snow. This predator is only slightly larger than a dog, but dogs, being its favourite food, have to be protected from it.

Ordinary dogs freeze in fear when they see hyenas and are easily dragged away. Extraordinary dogs, like Alsatians and mountain dogs, put up a fight but are ultimately defeated. Leaving her four- or five-day-old pups, Lucy once more started her trips to the shop.

One evening, Lucy went at twilight and did not return. On snowy days, heavy darkness descends at dusk, and the air grows so heavy with frost that it cannot carry smells. Because of this, dogs' sense of smell diminishes in winter. They fail to detect hyenas approaching and easily fall prey to them. Next morning, the sight of several small and big paw prints and signs of dragging and being dragged backward and forward on the snow made it evident that Lucy had given up her life only after an extended battle. The moist marks of blood on the snow looked as if a child had upset a pot of red ink on a white page of its drawing book.

Everyone wept for Lucy, but the infant who should have wept the most knew nothing of what had happened. His eyes had opened the previous day, so he cried more for milk than for his mother. He was fed with milk made from milk powder, but even under a quilt, he kept searching for the warmth of his mother's belly and wailing aloud. Finally, we put him in a basket with soft wool and a half-knitted sweater, where he went to sleep in the imagined comfort of his mother's nearness. He looked like a ball of wool in the basket.

When I returned to Prayag, I had to bring him with me. When he grew up, he looked unusual, as his mother had. Born of a mountain dog father and an Alsatian mother, his mixed varna resulted in his looking like neither an Alsatian nor a mountain dog.

His brown, yellow and black hairs created a mingled hue that was like sunlight and shade. One colour as the sun rose, another in shadows and a third in broad daylight. There was a novelty in the width and sharpness of his ears too. The top of his head was bigger and broader than that of most dogs, and his face longer but well-shaped. His tail was thick like that of Alsatians but it coiled upward. His legs were long like those of Alsatians, but his paws were strong and broad like those of a mountain dog and his nails were curved. His body was broad above, but his slender belly aided his light and fast gait. His eyes were neither black nor brown nor light in hue. Those round eyes, tipped with black, were the colour of honey, like liquid gold in the light and transparent like frozen honey in the dark.

In keeping with his special looks, his strength and nature were special too. He could clear a high wall in one jump. He had a deep, slow, resounding voice. One bark at night would shake the still atmosphere. He completely lacked the natural qualities of ordinary dogs—constant eagerness for food, wagging the tail to show pleasure, licking to express gratitude, following the master with the humility of a petitioner, barking or biting for no reason.

I have observed and raised many dogs, but Neelu is the only one I have known who was free of the humility of dogs and had a pride uncharacteristic of them. If even the food he most liked was thrown to him disrespectfully, he would not look at it, let alone eat it.

If he was ever scolded, he wouldn't come into my presence without a great deal of cajoling.

For twelve years, the place he preferred to sit was the outside veranda of my house. He sat on the topmost step in front of the portico and inspected all who came and went. He recognized most of my acquaintances. On seeing a special friend, he would gravely walk in and stand at the door of my room. His coming in this way would alert me that a friend had arrived. When he heard me say, 'I'm coming,' he would return to his place outside and sit down there.

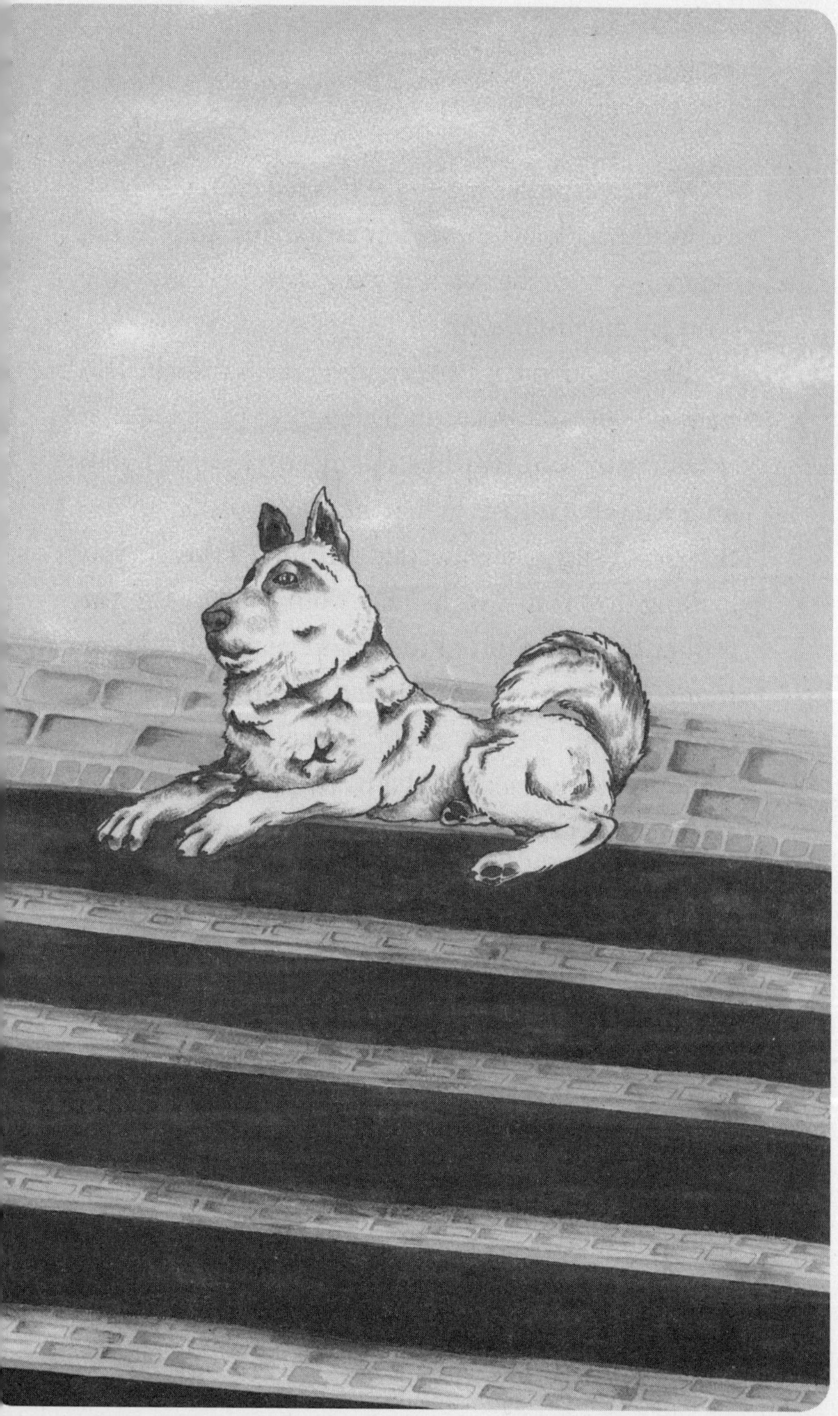

When an unknown or unexpected visitor arrived, he would look on in an impassive and indifferent manner while the person rang the bell and the servant came to inform me.

Dogs understand tones, not words. Neelu had such a wide and deep understanding of tones that speaking to him was like talking to a person who understands words. When he was outside or on the path, and someone said to him, 'Guru-ji was looking for you, Neelu,' he would leap over the wall at the speed of lightning and stand outside my room, waiting for a command. Until I said, 'Go, there's nothing to be done,' he would stand there like a statue. Sometimes I'd be busy with some task and wouldn't realize he was there, so he would have to wait, motionless, for a long time.

Despite being the son of a violent and fierce mountain dog father and a hunt-loving Alsatian mother, he had no tendency towards violence. In his long life of thirteen years, he was never seen pouncing on or killing any animal or bird. This temperament surprised both me and many other observers.

Sparrows often build nests in the skylights of my bungalow. I do not like to break the nests they laboriously build, so after a while their world of eggs and nestlings takes form there. As soon as bud-like wings sprout, the fledgelings fall from the skylights in their unsuccessful attempts to fly. At such times, Neelu became their alert guardian. For fear of him, no cat or dog dared harm those flying and falling innocents. Sometimes, to get very small nestlings restored to their nest, he would bring them to me, holding them gently in his mouth. Until I arranged for a ladder to be brought and the baby bird to be put back in the nest, he would either hold it tenderly in his mouth or else put it in my hand and then stand, waiting.

When I went out every morning to feed the peacocks, rabbits and others in the aviary, he would meet me at the door and accompany me, regardless of cold or rain. The aviary has a net screen above a two-foot-high wall. Neelu would stand with his forepaws on the wall and cast his round eyes about to inspect every aperture and its inhabitants. This routine of his never varied.

His nightly routine was also self-arranged and precise. When everyone had gone to sleep, he would sit out on the lawn in summer and on the veranda in winter, guarding the house. Several times a night, he would walk around the entire compound and the aviary. Whether the night was moonlit or thunderous, and even if there was a storm, he never halted his perambulations. In the silence of the night, we could tell by his deep, solemn voice which part of the grounds he was guarding.

Rabbits dig long, tunnel-like burrows with openings at both ends. One night, my rabbits dug a burrow that opened into my neighbour's compound, and several of them who were the leaders of this campaign were torn to pieces by a wild tomcat. The rabbits inside the burrow could not know the fate of those who emerged from it, so coming out one after another, they would all have become the prey of a cat or jackal. But, fortunately for them, Neelu, on his usual rounds, was perhaps alerted by the rustling of leaves and must have looked over the wall and seen the endangered rabbits in the dim moonlight of the frosty winter night.

As soon as he leapt over the wall, the cat fled, but he stood all night at the burrow's opening, getting drenched in dew, in order to prevent the rabbits from leaving the burrow.

Neelu paid a high price for this benevolence because he caught a chill and then pneumonia and had to endure the pain of injections and medications for many days. He drank bitter medicine and bore injections with patience.

Once, when I was injured in a car accident and had to go straight to hospital from the roadway, he understood, after waiting all day for me and observing the agitation of those who took clothes, sheets, blankets, and other goods to hospital for me, that something untoward had happened.

All those who visited my bungalow that evening were struck by Neelu's silent, grieving demeanour.

When he refused to eat or drink for three days, the doctor's permission was sought to bring him to the hospital.

He walked around the bed to view me properly in the swathes of bandages and then, reassured, took up his usual guardian position under my bed. It was only after much coaxing and cajoling that, two hours later, he agreed to go home.

After that, if he was not taken to the hospital every alternate day, he would begin fasting. Thus, he became one of my regular visitors at the hospital, and all the doctors and nurses got to know him.

Neelu's allotted lifespan was fourteen years, and from birth, up to the moment of his death, he was with me, so I have many memories of incidents connected with him.[1]

Among the dogs, only the company of Kajli pleased him, but Kajli and Badal could not be parted for even a moment. As a result, poor Neelu remained solitary.

Like his life, his death too was free of abjection. To die a dog's death is proverbial, but if anyone can face death in Neelu's calm, unattached manner, such a death would be desirable for a human being.

I have many living creatures, but now there is none regarding whom I have to worry that they might take offence.

Notes

1. Earlier, Mahadevi writes that he lived for thirteen years.

Nikki, Rosie, and Rani

Perception is present in childhood memories as water is in drenched clothing. It is not directly visible, but it is continuously expressed in the cool touch of the clothing. Another peculiarity of these memories is that as they recede in time, they draw closer.

The lines that gather varied colours and emerge in their full significance from the mists of my childhood are based, among other things, on three beings who, though not members of the human community, are, as it were, imprinted on my memory. Nikki the mongoose, Rosie the bitch and Rani the mare.

As soon as Rosie's eyes opened, some princely student of my father's gave her to me as a present on my fifth birthday. It was natural for us both to grow up together. Rosie drank milk with me, slept on my cot, rode on my wooden horse and joined my games. My love of animals can be said to have begun with Rosie's companionship, which remained unbroken for thirteen long years.

Rosie was white, but the tips of her small, well-shaped ears, the tip of her tail, the centre of her forehead and her forepaws were dark red, which suggested the colouring of a white sari with a red border. She was of the small but fierce terrier tribe; partly because of her nature and partly because of our companionship, she developed some characteristics rarely found in dogs, which led to her getting the same kind of affection in our house as children did. We all accepted her as a companion without whom we could not go anywhere or eat anything.

At that time, my father was vice principal of Daly College in Indore, and we lived in the cantonment, where there was no neighbouring settlement.[1] Tutors came morning and evening to teach us. The afternoons were free but were extremely busy for us.

My youngest brother was too small to join in this busy routine, but I, my younger sister and the brother younger than her spent the afternoons roaming around, breaking weaver birds' nests and collecting dried acacia pods inside which seeds rattled. We were equally busy and active when the air stood still in summer, when the atmosphere seemed to melt and pour in the rainy season and when time seemed to freeze in winter.

When we needed to rest from our wanderings, our favourite resting place was a dried-up tank surrounded by mango trees. Its upper slopes were eight to nine feet high in the shadow of the trees, and it was four to five feet deep in the open sunshine. Many branches of the mango trees swung and dipped over the dried-up tank. Withered leaves had filled up several feet of the dry depths. We three would swing on the branches or else, like Robinson Crusoe, would keep measuring the depths of the island in our flat ocean. In our peregrinations, if we came across a sunberry plant or a corinda bush covered with berries, we felt as if we were in the Nandanvan forest.[2]

Rosie always accompanied us on these journeys. When we sat and swung on the branches, she sat below our feet on the brink of the slope, waiting for the command to leap in. When we circumambulated the tank, she ran ahead as if to show us the way, and when we collected sunberries and corinda berries, she would sit, uninterested, in the shade of a bush. In the summer, when small or big mangoes were blown down into the tank, Rosie would jump in and fish them out from the sea of rustling leaves. The poor thing's small, pink mouth would get stained by raw mangoes, but this did not deter her search.

In the afternoons, my father would be at college and my mother busy with household tasks or looking after our youngest brother. Rama would depart for the market, and Kallu's mother would either take a nap or else set herself to scrubbing the pots and pans till they shone. They all thought we were either sleeping or studying in our rooms. But we would first lower Rosie from the window, and then one by one descend from the window into the garden and skulk through the corinda bushes until we got to that deserted world of freedom. It was not safe for any one of us to be left behind because he or she could become an informer if bribed with biscuits or sweets. It was, therefore, necessary for all three to go. Rosie had been initiated into our secret society, so she accompanied us. She had understood the mysteries of our campaign so well that as soon as it was afternoon, she would grow anxious to jump out of the window, and when lowered down, would sit below, eagerly watching us descend. When we jumped out of the window, one of us would sometimes fall on her, but she considered it against the rules to make the slightest sound.

After one such unrestrained excursion, while we were swinging from the mango tree's boughs and inspecting our treasures, we heard a mango fall. Rosie jumped down. She kept searching for something among the leaves for some time, and then we were astonished to see her emerge, holding a living creature in her mouth. A mongoose couple had constructed a burrow in the slope of that dried-up pond and had begun to actively contribute to the work of the lord of all beings. A tiny member of their mongoose world, an anarchist like us, had sneaked away from his creators and swum to the surface of the sea of dead leaves. As soon as he lifted his little face above the leaves and cast a wondering eye on the world outside, he found himself in the small, dark cavity of Rosie's mouth. Rosie was so experienced at fetching us raw mangoes without marking them with her teeth that she safely brought the whimpering little creature to us.

He was no larger than a squirrel but very different in appearance. His shiny brown hue, black and red eyes, soft paws, tiny pink mouth, and minute shell-like ears hidden in fur made him seem like a little living toy to us. Rosie had held him gently, but his struggles had resulted in a few scratches. Now he lay unmoving from extreme fear of being hurt. We were so pleased to have him that we ran home, leaving behind our collection of nests, smooth stones, wild oleander flowers, and so on. In the excitement of the moment, we forgot that our wanderings were supposed to be clandestine. But mother did not ask where and how we had found that tiny being. After giving us a long sermon about not harassing animals, she told us to return him to the burrow of his mongoose parents.

We felt deep sympathy for the infant mongoose. We could guess the hardship for a child who had to sit day and night in a small burrow in his parents' presence. If our father were to make us sit in front of him in a small room night and day and keep teaching us while our mother sat nearby stitching and knitting, how would we feel? Some such unpleasant condition must have prevailed in the burrow otherwise why would such a small child run away! We went unwillingly in search of the mongoose baby's burrow and of his parents, inhabitants of the burrow, and having failed in our search, returned more pleased than disappointed.

Now that little creature had no refuge except us. We happily emptied our small toy box and lined it with cotton wool and a silk handkerchief. Then, with many pleadings and promises to obey all his orders, we persuaded Rama to feed him milk with a cotton-wool wick. Thus, the smallest member was inducted into our small family.

When he grew healthy and strong in a few days, thanks to Rama's watchful care, and became a discerning companion of ours, we forgot the promise we had given Rama and became as undisciplined as we were before.

Mother named him Nakul, which was the modern form of the Sanskrit name for his species, but following a tendency to abbreviate, we began to call him Nikki.

As a pet, a mongoose is very affectionate and disciplined. Nourished by anything that a squirrel will eat, such as insects, moths, fruit, flowers, he can stay with his human companions all day and night. In a pocket, on a shoulder, in a sleeve, in hair, wherever he is placed, he sits quietly, looking around and evaluating his surroundings with playful but alert eyes.

Nikki always stayed with me.

In those days, small girls in our family were dressed in *gharara*, kurta, and dupatta, all with decorative borders, in which they looked like small editions of medieval begums. Sometimes, to indicate progressiveness, they were also put into frocks with collars, lace and fringes, canopied in which they appeared like companions to Queen Victoria, thus representing East and West together. Our shoes, too, were divided into eastern and western ones. When in eastern dress we slid along in small, light, gold-embroidered *jooti*, and when in western dress, we tottered about in high-heeled, laced shoes, with black or white socks that came up above our knees. Mind and feet both revolted against these modes of movement, because they allowed us neither to climb over corinda bushes nor to run.

Therefore, we would hide both types of footwear in the cupboard, jump out of the window and race barefoot over pebbles and stones.

Nikki would either swing in a fold of my dupatta or hide behind my neck in my braid, from where his tiny face would peer out near my ear and survey everything that was going on all around. Rosie's job was to run along with us, but Nikki would jump out of his safe spot and run only when he felt like it. One day, just as we descended from the window, Nikki's sharp eyes spotted a long, black snake in the grass near the rose bed, and he sprang towards it. We were astonished to see Nikki standing on his hind legs as if challenging the snake, and the snake hissing, half-risen in the air.

Thinking that the snake had killed Nikki, we all started screaming, yelling and throwing stones at the snake. Had Rama not appeared in response to the hullaballoo, the outcome could have been unfortunate.

That day we realized for the first time that our Nikki, no larger than the span of a hand, could fight with a snake that was several feet long. The fight between them was like the play of lightning with the swaying bough of a tree. Nikki described circles around the snake at such speed that he looked like a rotating brown blot. The snake kept striking with its hood, hissing and moving backwards and forwards, trying to wrap him in its coils, but could not manage to catch Nikki, who was flashing around like lightning. Leaping up with tremendous speed, he kept attacking the snake beneath its hood with his sharp teeth.

Thanks to Rama, we were not able to stay outside to watch the finale of this untimely battle, but when Nikki came and sat at the window, we looked out and saw the snake cut into several pieces. Afraid that there might be poison on Nikki's mouth, Rama submerged his face in water and washed it repeatedly and then gave him milk to drink.

Although it has the power to cut to pieces a poisonous snake, a mongoose is entirely devoid of poison. In the world of living beings, non-poisonous creatures are killed by poisonous ones and those who are more poisonous defeat those who are less poisonous. But the mongoose is an exception.

Although non-poisonous, a mongoose does not die of a snake's poison nor is it defeated in battle with a poisonous creature.

A mongoose is fragile and light compared to a snake. A snake could easily crush it in its coils or strike it unconscious with its hood. But the mongoose's flower-like lightness and lightning speed defeat the snake. The mongoose does not give it the opportunity to strike or the time to construct a coil. And because of its smallness, the mongoose does not need an especially favourable opportunity.

In the meanwhile, my father decided to enrol me in the mission school in the city. This plan bid fair to put an end to all our projects, so we were deeply troubled and anxious, but we were helpless.

Finally, one day, clutching my books, I was compelled to climb into a covered vehicle, a *shikram*, which was a sign of high status in the city in those days, and set out.

Nikki was with me, as always, though my father had given orders that he must be left at home. When we reached the mission school, I found that he was sitting on the roof of the vehicle. I succeeded in hiding him in my clothes and taking him inside.

But the commotion that ensued when he was seen with me in the classroom stupefied me and rendered me speechless. '*She has brought a reptile! Throw it away,*'[3] shrieked the sisters and my classmates. I knew the meaning of the word 'reptile', but I understood that it was meant as an insult to Nikki. In a somewhat displeased fashion, I repeatedly stated that this was my Nikki and that he never bit anyone. Despite this, no one was willing to sit with him. Having no option, I seated him in a creeper that overspread the gate and the walls, but I was so worried about losing him that I could not concentrate on my work.

When I was leaving, and Nikki leapt down on to my shoulder, my eyes filled with tears of joy. This became our daily routine.

Rama came every day to drop me off and pick me up, and he was favourably inclined to Nikki on account of having nurtured him, so on the journey, Nikki would sit on my lap. While I was in school, he spent his time scurrying around in the creeper in the mission compound or wandering the garden. His jumping down on my shoulder when I reached the gate after school ended was so well regulated that he never delayed me by even a few minutes.

The atmosphere in the mission was different from that at home. The style of dressing was different, the way of praying was different, the pictures and statues were different, even God's name was different and the biggest difference was that Nikki was forbidden to enter there.

After this, the biggest of our animals joined the family.

As a princely state, Indore had an abundance of majestic horses and vehicles. Also, we used to see English children riding about on small ponies, which were white donkeys (Rama had enlightened us about the lineages of these animals). In Rama's stories, kings would seat criminals on donkeys and banish them from the country. Seeing the children happily riding about on donkeys, it was hard to believe that they were being punished. Rama had the answer to our questions. In their foreign country, the punishment of riding a donkey was meted out to them, and they were sent to India to suffer this punishment because donkeys are not found in England.

One day, the three of us submitted an oral memorandum to father, stating that our not having a small horse was an injustice. If other children had the right to ride horses, we should have this right too.

Laughing, father asked, 'Do you want to sit on a white pony?' After much tussling and whispers of 'You say,' 'You say,' I stepped forward and solemnly replied, 'White ponies are donkeys and sitting on them is a punishment.'

I don't know whether or not father rebuked Rama, our perennial fount of knowledge, but after a few days, we saw a small, chocolate-coloured pony tethered in the western veranda of the courtyard. The veranda was not made for tethering ponies, so a new door was constructed in the wall for the pony to be brought in and out, and a syce named Chhuttan was employed to take charge of massaging, feeding, watering, and exercising the pony.

We were greatly impressed by the small pony and somewhat afraid of it. No change in the house had been made for us or for our other companion animals nor had any special servant been employed. Rama could not be called a servant because apart from scolding us severely, he also pulled our ears. And we had not been able to get our window changed into a door, which would have saved us the inconvenience of having to jump down with Rosie and Nikki. Even though father told us that the pony had been brought for us to ride, we continued to be displeased and annoyed with her for four or five days, but after that she won our friendship. We asked Rama the pony's name and were told that she was called Tajrani. We had seen pictures of the Taj Mahal, and having heard all about the joys and sorrows of queens in Rama's and Kallu Ma's stories, we were deeply sympathetic to her. Even though she was the queen of a building like the Taj Mahal, she had been sent away from there—imagining this melted our jealousy and anger into compassion and we began to devise ways to make her more comfortable.

She was so beautiful that her image is still imprinted on my eyes. A light chocolatey, shiny colour, on which one's vision seemed to slip and slide. A forelock swung between her small, upstanding ears, her eyes were large, black, clean, and seemingly transparent, and she had red nostrils which she kept swelling out to snuff up scents on all sides. One could glimpse the shining teeth and red tongue in her long, pink-lipped mouth, which was not wounded even though she had to keep chewing iron. Her back was broad and disproportionate to her height. Her legs were strong and shapely, and her thick tail kept falling and rising like a peacock-feather fan, swishing away flies. At that time, I did not have the wisdom to understand all these details but even after such a long time, those lineaments arise on the tablet of memory, as letters written with invisible ink emerge when heated by fire.

We kept wondering why she was not just a little smaller. Had she been smaller we could have kept her in our room like Rosie and Nikki.

It was not possible to take Rani to our room, so the veranda-turned-stable became the headquarters of our anarchy. The veranda had not been made for tethering a horse, so there were several shelves and niches and an open cupboard in its walls. The family of our voluntarily displaced as well as refugee toys took up their abode there.

Swinging on Rani's neck, putting flowers in her ears and mane and feeding her biscuits and sweets, we soon established such a friendship with her that she would grow uneasy, stamp her feet and start whinnying when she didn't see us around.

Then began our training in riding. Ordinary but good-looking jeans were bought for my sister and me and heavily pleated leather jeans for my brother, which would protect him from falling even if he lost his balance.

We would stand on the platform outside and take turns to climb on Rani's back. Chhuttan would take us out and run alongside. In the mornings, my brother and sister rode, and when I returned from school, the programme would be repeated in the late afternoon or evening.

But how could our rebellious natures be satisfied with this kind of riding? Nor were we content with simply swinging on Rani's neck or climbing on her back by using a stool in her stable.

Finally, one holiday afternoon, when everyone was asleep, we untethered Rani, took her out, climbed on to her bare back from the platform and turn by turn gave evidence of completing our incomplete education.

It was natural for Tajrani to be influenced by our anarchic tendencies. Children do not perceive different levels of consciousness; they perceive just one consciousness. For them, animals, birds and plants all belong to one family.

Nikki would swing on Rani's tail, Rosie would leap on to her back and then leap down, and all of us would sit on her back as proudly as if we were installed on a peacock throne.

Rani knew the strengths and weaknesses of all of us. She would satisfy those who sat on her bare back and clung to her mane, by gently trotting around with them. But one day when I was sitting on her, my brother hit her legs with a thin cane he had in his hand. There was no possibility of her getting hurt, but perhaps her dignity was wounded, or some bad memory was aroused. She ran as fast as if the road, the trees, the river, the ditches, all had resolved to catch hold of her and tie her up.

For a while, I managed to remain seated on that flying saucer, but my falling was inevitable. As soon as I fell, Rani seemed to come back from the past to the present and stood as still as if she were a petrified image of penance.

Everyone ran out, hearing my companions' screams, and I had to spend many days in bed.

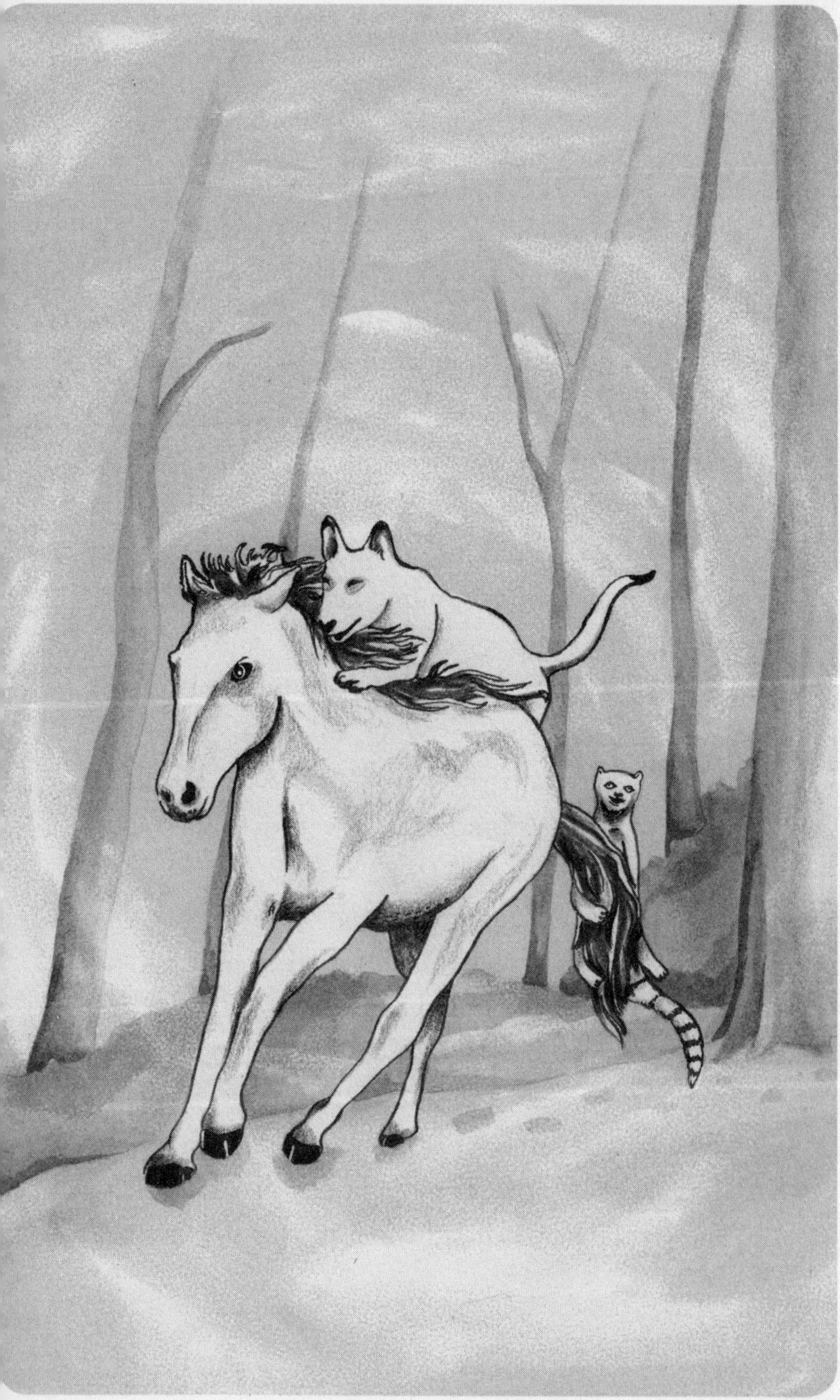

When I recovered and went to see Rani, she looked at me so repentantly and whinnied in such a way that tears came to my eyes.

Once, on my brother's birthday, our grandmother sent gold bracelets for him. Usually, whenever we wore new clothes or ornaments, we went to show them to Rani. My brother went to see her, wearing the beautiful, snake-headed bracelets, and who knows what inspired him to take them both off and put them like rings around her alert, upstanding ears.

Then we all got busy playing and forgot about the bracelets. In the evening, my mother saw my brother's bare arms, inquired, and set a search in motion. But the bracelets were not to be found anywhere.

Rani kept digging in one corner with her hooves and neighing. Finally, Father noticed and told Chhuttan to clear the mud from that corner. Someone had dug a hole there and buried the bracelets. Nobody was punished for this, but Rani won a place in everyone's heart.

One incident is memorable for its strangeness. One morning, when we woke up, we saw a small horse with Rani. 'Where did he come from?' we kept asking until Rama got so fed up that he announced that the new creature had been eating and sleeping in Rani's stomach. Brother enthusiastically asked, 'Are there more of them?' and Rama nodded his head in the affirmative.

Now we were wonderstruck but also angered. These small creatures do no work but they lie in the stomach of Rani, who runs about with us on her back, and they eat up her food.

Brother said that we should cut open Rani's stomach and take out at least one more such foal. Then he and my younger sister could ride on the foals, and Rani would be just for me. The proposal seemed appropriate to me, but when, one afternoon, he brought the vegetable-cutting knife, my courage ran out. Our attention was drawn to another problem. How would we sew up Rani's stomach? Mother's delicate needle would not work. Rama kept a big needle in his room to sew sacking, but we couldn't get hold of that. After some days, when Rani's foal grew big enough to run around, we forgot both our anger and our project.

Then, suddenly, the tempest of revolution destroyed our anarchic kingdom, and we were exiled to the country of sensible people. When we returned home from vacation, Nikki had died, and Rani and her son Pavan had been given away. Only Rosie, weak, lonely, and lost, pressed against our legs and whimpered sadly.

Notes

1. Indore was a Maratha state, ruled by the Holkars. Daly College was a public school for children of royalty and nobility, both Hindu and Muslim. It is one of the oldest co-educational schools in the world.
2. In the epics and Puranas, Nandanvan is the delightful forest of Indra. The name means 'joy-giving'.
3. These words are in English in the original.

A Note on the Author and the Translator

MAHADEVI VARMA was born on Holi in 1907. She did an MA in Sanskrit from Allahabad University and became residential principal (later, vice chancellor) of the pioneering women's institution, Prayag Mahila Vidyapeeth. She worked in the Gandhi-led movement for independence, and edited several journals, most notably the women's magazine *Chand*. She was one of the four pillars of the Chhayavad movement in Hindi poetry and the author of several collections of poems, such as *Nihar* (1930), *Rashmi* (1932), *Nirja* (1933), *Yama* (1939), and *Deepshikha* (1942). She wrote several prose works, including reminiscences, pen portraits (*Ateet ke Chalchitra*, 1941; *Smriti ki Rekhayen*, 1943; *Path ke Sathi*, 1946), essays on women's predicament (*Shrinkhla ki Kariyan*, 1942), and works of literary criticism, such as *Sahityakar ki Astha* (1962). She translated numerous works from Sanskrit to Hindi.

Mahadevi founded a trust to support writers in need. In 1979, she was the first woman to be made a fellow of the Sahitya Akademi. Among other awards, she received the Jnanpith in 1982, the Padma Bhushan in 1956, and the Padma Vibhushan posthumously in 1988. She died in 1987.

RUTH VANITA, former reader in English at Miranda House and later in the English department, Delhi University, is professor of English at the University of Montana. She is the author of many books, including the novel *Memory of Light*; *Love's Rite: Same-Sex Marriages in Modern India*; *Gender, Sex and the City: Urdu Rekhti Poetry 1780–1870*; and *Dancing with the Nation: Courtesans in Bombay Cinema*, and of over seventy essays on British and Indian literature. She was co-founder of *Manushi*, India's first nationwide feminist magazine, which she co-edited for thirteen years.

Vanita co-edited the pioneering *Same-Sex Love in India: A Literary History*, and has translated many works from Hindi to English, including the stories of Premchand and novels by Rajendra Yadav and Mannu Bhandari. Her forthcoming book is *The Dharma of Justice in the Sanskrit Epics: Debates on Gender, Varna and Species*. She divides her time between Missoula and Gurgaon.

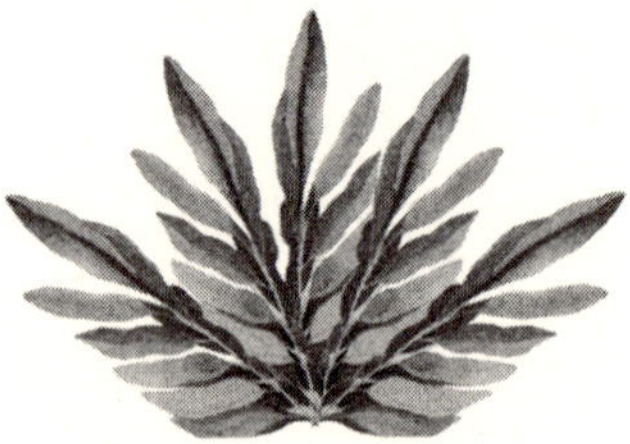